"What's going on with you and Danny?" Alex asked, her voice trembling.

Stephanie's eyes narrowed. "I don't know what you're talking about. Nothing's *going on* between Danny and me."

"I don't believe you."

"Believe what you like." She yawned, lazily picking a pine needle from her hair. "Why should I care?"

Alex felt dizzy with anger. Heat climbed into her face. Even the roots of her hair felt as if they were on fire.

"That's right," she replied bitterly. "I should have remembered. You don't care about anything. Or anyone."

"What difference would it make?" Stephanie demanded. Her voice cracked, becoming slightly shrill. "No one ever cared about me!"

# SENIORS

TOO MUCH, TOO SOON
SMART ENOUGH TO KNOW
WINNER ALL THE WAY
AFRAID TO LOVE
BEFORE IT'S TOO LATE
TOO HOT TO HANDLE
HANDS OFF, HE'S MINE

# HANDS OFF, HE'S MINE
## by Eileen Goudge

LAUREL-LEAF BOOKS

Published by Dell Publishing Co., Inc.
1 Dag Hammarskjold Plaza
New York, New York 10017

Created by Cloverdale Press
133 Fifth Avenue
New York, New York 10003

Cover photo by Pat Hill

Laurel-Leaf Library ® TM 766734.
Dell Publishing Co., Inc.

Seniors™ is a trademark of Dell Publishing Co., Inc.,
New York, New York.

ISBN: 0-440-93359-5

RL: 5.2

Printed in the United States of America

First printing—June 1985

To Kathee Card, a friend for all seasons.

# CHAPTER ONE

"Okay, I'll let you have it easy this time . . . since you're a boy." Alex was grinning as she lobbed the ball over the net, but she gave it all she had.

Forty, love. One more point and the game would be hers.

Danny loped across the court in two easy strides. His sweat-shined brown arm flashed, scooping her serve with an effortless stroke. Too effortless. The ball sailed up and over the net in a leisurely arc—a perfect white bull's-eye punched in the sheet of blue sky.

Alex charged the net, her eyes never leaving the target above. In one fluid motion, she swung her racket. There was the whiffle of air through taut cat-

1

gut as she struck. *Thwock.* She felt the impact travel up her forearm, spreading through her in an electric wave, as she smashed the ball onto Danny's court just inches from the net.

Back at the baseline, Danny made no attempt to return it. He merely shrugged, watching it dribble out of bounds. Alex stared at him, frustration welling up inside her.

"You didn't even *try*," she scolded as he trotted up to the net. His tanned face shone with sweat, and his sun-streaked hair had separated into damp spikes at his temples. "You could've gone after it."

Danny grinned. "I thought this was a game, not total annihilation."

He dropped his racket and brought his large hands to rest on her shoulders. Alex could feel the dampness of his palms through her T-shirt. She shivered with pleasure, tilting her head back to meet his amused gaze. Darn him! He never took her seriously. He never took *anything* seriously.

But she couldn't resist the magnetic pull of those sparkling blue eyes. Danny's warmth and humor drew her in like a safe harbor whenever her own emotions became choppy. Wasn't that what had attracted her to him in the first place, despite how really different they were? They'd been going together almost a whole year—since they were juniors—and she still melted whenever he smiled that heart-stopping grin of his.

Alex sighed. "You could be the best tennis player at Glenwood, if you gave it all your energy."

"Who says I want to be the best? Go pick on Jimmy Connors." He laughed, immune to her goading. "Maybe you'd like him to be your boyfriend. Only I doubt if even *he* could keep up with you."

"You nut . . . aren't you ever serious?"

"Not if I can help it."

Alex groaned. Danny had the same attitude about diving. As long as they'd been on the team together, she'd been encouraging him to practice more, to develop his competitive edge. You really had to hustle if you wanted to make it to the top, and while Danny was a good diver, he was far too laid back. He was always telling *her* she should relax more. As if she could and still be number one!

It wasn't just sports, either. Danny was that way about most things. Take college, for instance. He'd applied to several, but he really didn't care which one he went to, just as long as he was accepted by at least one school. He didn't have any particular goal yet for the future, so it didn't really matter. He'd thought about going into computers, he said, but it was just a thought—he didn't want to lock himself into anything at the moment.

Danny hooked an arm about her neck as they strolled off the court. He was just four inches taller than Alex, so her shoulder tucked neatly into the curve of his armpit.

He looked down at her, a quizzical line forming between his eyebrows. "Forget about me. What's with *you* today? You went after that ball like a kamikaze pilot."

Alex giggled. "None of your dumb Japanese jokes, *puh-leez.*"

Danny was always teasing her, in a nice way, about being half-Japanese—telling her she'd look great dressed in a kimono; or, like the time they were studying World War II in American history, when he joked that if the Japanese had had her on their side, they probably would've won.

She always threw it back at Danny by calling him the all-American white-bread hero. It was a lot of silliness. Except for her straight dark hair and almond-shaped eyes, Alex was no more ethnic than he was. Though proud of her Japanese heritage, she didn't even know how to eat with chopsticks.

The truth was, they were far more different on the inside than on the surface. That's why they teased each other so much. It was one way they could air their differences without hurting each other.

"I guess I *am* sort of uptight," she admitted.

She bent down to gather up the balls that had collected alongside the fence, shoving them into their empty can. It was early in the morning, so the tennis courts were empty. The only movement was a cat slinking along the scarred base of the backboard. When it saw Alex and Danny, it froze, then darted off into the trees.

Alex found the plastic cover to her racket on the bench beside the backboards. She zipped it on, then sat down, pulling her leg up to tighten the lace on her sneaker.

"I don't blame you," Danny said, softening. "I'd be uptight, too. Wow, I can hardly believe today is the big day."

"I couldn't sleep last night. I was all tied up, wondering what she'll be like." Alex could feel her stomach clench even as she said it. She leaped up and started heading up the hill toward the parking lot.

Danny fell into step beside her. "It does seem

strange—having someone you've never even met for a sister."

"*Foster* sister," she corrected. "Yeah, it does seem weird, doesn't it? But the agency says it's better this way. Picking a kid isn't supposed to be like squeezing grapefruits in the supermarket. You have to make the commitment, no matter what the kid's going to be like."

"Well, she's our age—that's one thing you have in common."

"I just hope that's not all."

Danny grinned. "Look at us. We're the original Odd Couple, and we get along pretty well most of the time."

"Says who!" Alex playfully swung her racket at him.

Danny neatly sidestepped it, darting around in back of her. In a flash, he'd pinned her arms against her sides in a ferocious bear hug. The harder she struggled to free herself, the tighter he squeezed. Alex could feel the hard bands of his muscles as they flexed against her. His breath came in uneven, laughing gusts against her ear.

Suddenly they were both laughing too hard to fight. Alex collapsed back against him, holding her stomach. Danny loosened his grasp and began nibbling on her neck.

"Mmm. You taste good."

"You're weird, you know that?" She twisted around to face him, reaching up to rumple his hair.

"I know. It's one of the reasons you're so madly attracted to me, right?"

"Right." She grinned, too out of breath for laughter. "Besides the charge I get from beating you at tennis."

Danny grabbed her by the wrist, holding her arm

5

aloft. "Supergirl! No man can stand up against her. She's faster than a speeding bullet . . ."

Alex felt her laughter fizzle. She sensed an edge to Danny's kidding that she didn't like. "Danny, cut it out."

". . . more powerful than a locomotive . . ."

"Danny, I mean it."

". . . able to leap tall buildings at a single bound . . ."

"Danny!"

He stopped. "Sorry. Guess I just got carried away." That was the trouble with all their kidding; sometimes it got out of hand.

Alex was sorry, too. She shouldn't have snapped at him like that. Besides, she was the one who had started it.

"We'd better get going if we want to stop for a doughnut on the way home," she said. "I promised Dad I wouldn't be too long. He wants to get an early start. The place where we're picking up Stephanie is all the way over in San Jose."

They linked arms and continued up the hill. Alex was wearing her favorite orange jogging shorts and baggy Glenwood T-shirt. The breeze was cool against her sweaty skin. She felt energized from her workout, and from being with Danny—strong enough to face anything now.

Well, *almost* anything. She still couldn't help feeling nervous, wondering what it would be like to have a foster sister. This was sure to be a different kind of challenge from the ones she was constantly imposing on herself. A lot depended on Stephanie, too. What would she be like? Would she want to be a part of their

6

family—or would she resent them in some strange way?

Alex longed to confide all her fears to Danny, but she held back. Danny would be sympathetic, of course, but he just wouldn't be able to relate to those kinds of anxieties. He just naturally expected everything to work out, and usually, because he was so easy-going, it did. He'd never worry about whether or not Stephanie would like him, if she were going to be *his* foster sister. He would take it for granted that they'd get along. As long as he liked somebody, why shouldn't they like him back?

She remembered when Doug Spaulding had moved next door to Danny last year. Doug had been a real troublemaker, whose parents, in desperation, had sent him away from home to live with his aunt and uncle with the hope that he would straighten out. At first, it hadn't looked as if he would. Doug was always in trouble at school, and he got picked up by the police once for driving without a license.

It was Danny who decided that Doug was just lonely and trying to get attention any way he could. So he started offering Doug rides to school in the morning, and in no time the two of them were hanging out together at home and around campus. Pretty soon, Doug straightened out. He began concentrating on his schoolwork and even got on the basketball team.

When Alex asked Danny what miracle he had worked on Doug, Danny merely shrugged and said, "There was nothing really wrong with old Doug. He just needed someone to talk to."

Friendships were never that simple for Alex. She was outgoing and had never had any trouble making friends, but unlike Danny, she expected a lot from other people—almost as much as she expected from herself. Sometimes this got her into trouble. She always meant well, but the more you expect from someone, she'd found, the more you set yourself up for disappointment.

Alex pulled apart from Danny, breaking into a run. They were near the top of the slope, where it looked out over the whole Glenwood High campus—a maze of low buildings connected by covered ramps. The wide lawns surrounding them were a lush green color, except in the places where herds of stampeding students had matted them into brown trails.

"Come on, you slowpoke!" she called back laughingly over her shoulder. "Last one up pays for the doughnuts!"

But her challenge didn't cause Danny to alter his easy, ambling pace one bit. He walked with one hand jammed into the pocket of his grass-streaked tennis shorts; with the other, he carried his tennis racket slung casually over one shoulder. His sun-gold hair fanned untidily over his forehead. She felt a flicker of frustration that bordered on annoyance.

Then he smiled—that impishly irresistible smile of his that spread up from the corners of his wide mouth, sparkling from his eyes—and her heart melted in spite of herself. He was Danny, and that's all that counted for the moment.

"Don't worry," she told him when he'd caught up with her. "I'm not really in the mood for doughnuts, anyway."

8

# CHAPTER TWO

Alex stared down the dim corridor, taking in the flaking green paint and barred windows. Even the overhead light fixture was imprisoned in wire netting. Cold horror washed through her. What kind of place *was* this?

Crestview Home for Girls. When she'd first heard the name she'd pictured something with curtains and lumpy couches, with girls squealing up and down the halls. Sort of like a dormitory, only nicer, homier. But this was . . . well, it just made her want to cry. To think that Stephanie actually *lived* here.

Alex could imagine how *she* would feel if she'd been dumped in this place like an abandoned kitten. To be locked away simply because you were homeless. It was so unfair!

"It's like a jail," she blurted out.

Mrs. Greenspan, the grim woman in charge of this floor, scowled at her. She had a hard, square face that didn't quite match her marshmallowy body, as if it had been stuck on as an afterthought.

Susan Enomoto slipped an arm about her daughter's shoulders. "It's only temporary, honey. That why they call it a detention center. Stephanie's only been here for three weeks."

Mom looked as perfectly composed as always. She'd had her hair done this morning while Alex was playing tennis. It was fluffed up in soft brownish-blond waves that made her roundish face look even rounder. She wore a ruffled peach-colored blouse with her good beige linen suit, which still looked unrumpled despite the long drive. But Alex could feel the tenseness in her mother's slender frame, drawn taut as a violin string.

Three weeks in this place would seem like three years, she thought. But she kept her mouth shut. Alex knew she had a bad habit of blurting out what was on her mind without really thinking. But, honestly, sometimes she just couldn't help it!

"Our security measures are mostly for the girls' own protection," Mrs. Greenspan explained, her stern expression unrelenting. "Most of them are runaways, like Stephanie. We're only making sure they stay put."

"Maybe if you made it a little homier—you know, with curtains and everything instead of just bars—then they'd *want* to stay," Alex suggested as nicely as possible.

Instantly, she could see it had been the wrong thing to say. Mrs. Greenspan pressed her lips together so tightly they looked as if they'd been drawn on with a very sharp red pencil. Even so, Alex wasn't sorry she'd said it.

Her father shot her a look of gentle reproach, but there was a spark of admiration in his dark eyes as well. Dad felt the same way she did, Alex was sure. He believed in standing up for what you thought was right and speaking out against what was wrong.

Alex felt proud, walking beside him. Everyone always said that they were alike. They certainly looked alike. She'd inherited his dark, Oriental features, if not his height. Dad was exceptionally tall for a Japanese man—over six feet.

"The other girls are downstairs in the rec hall right now," Mrs. Greenspan said, ignoring Alex's comment. She led the way down the corridor, past rows of locked, silent steel doors. "I've asked Stephanie to wait for you in her room. I thought it would be a good idea under the circumstances. These things are usually a little awkward at first."

"That was very considerate of you, Mrs. Greenspan," Susan replied graciously, as if that awful woman had done them a huge favor. Alex cringed inwardly.

Mrs. Greenspan softened a little, allowing a tiny smile to peep through her iron mask. Then she swept ahead of them, keys jangling at her hip, her squat heels hammering the scuffed linoleum floor.

Alex shivered, hunching her shoulders and drawing her hands in until they were nearly swallowed by the

11

sleeves of her baggy sweat shirt. It seemed cold, though it really wasn't. Outside the sun was shining. She knew it only seemed cold because she was so nervous.

What was it going to be like having a perfect stranger live with them? They'd been over it again and again—she, Mom, and Dad—discussing the advantages as well as the drawbacks, but what it really boiled down to was that none of them knew exactly what to expect. This was all so new to them, being a foster family. The only one who'd been through it before, who knew the rules—if there were any—was Stephanie.

Miss Bryson, the social worker, had warned them that Stephanie might seem withdrawn at first. She'd lived with five other foster families before and had run away from the last one. It might be awhile before she could learn to build up the kind of trust it would take to become actively involved with Alex's family.

Alex had tried to imagine what Stephanie would be like. They'd seen only one photograph of her—a school picture that had been taken in the ninth grade. You couldn't tell much from it. The photograph showed a thin face and brown hair sliding over one eye so that it looked as if she were peering out from a hiding place.

What had struck Alex most about that picture was that Stephanie hadn't been smiling. Not even a little bit. Alex always found it impossible to keep a straight face when they were taking her picture at school. Those photographers were always coaxing you to look happy, or say "cheese," or some dumb thing. Obviously, Stephanie wasn't used to giving in, even in small matters.

But then maybe that was because her life hadn't been easy. Miss Bryson had said that Stephanie was abandoned by her mother at the age of five. She didn't have a father, either. No real family at all, not even a sister or a brother.

An image of Noodle came to mind. Alex wished so much her brother could've been here. She could almost see him, skinny arms pumping as he rolled his wheelchair alongside them. Grinning that wide, lopsided grin that seemed to take up his whole face. He would've made a funny face behind old Greenspan's back, and Alex would've had to fight to keep from laughing out loud.

She missed him so much. Ever since he'd died, there had been this tender spot in her throat, and whenever she thought of Noodle, it ached. When it ached too badly, she couldn't keep from crying. But now wasn't the time for tears, she told herself. That would only make things twice as hard. None of them needed reminding that they probably wouldn't be here at all if Noodle were still alive.

Her brother's death had left an empty hole in their lives. But it was a place no one else could ever fill. The best she and her parents could offer Stephanie was a new start, a place of her own with people who wanted to love her. If she wanted to be part of their family, that is. And it was a big If, in Alex's opinion.

Mrs. Greenspan halted at the very end of the corridor, at the last door on the left. She didn't bother to knock; she just opened it with one sharp wrench. Stephanie could have been naked inside there, for all she cared.

Alex hung back, ashamed at being a part of this

intrusion. But the slim, brunette girl on the bed didn't seem to mind. She sat facing the window, staring out at the parking lot below. The small room was layered with haze from the cigarette she was smoking. She wore jeans and a crumpled denim jacket, but in spite of her offhanded appearance, Alex was struck by how pretty her new sister was.

It was an awkward moment, just standing there, waiting for this strange girl to stop pretending they didn't exist. Alex had never felt so uncomfortable in her life.

Languidly, as if she were arranging this introduction entirely on her terms, Stephanie yawned, then swiveled slowly about to face them. Her expression didn't change one bit. She might still have been staring at a row of parked cars for all the impact their arrival had apparently made on her.

Alex wouldn't have recognized Stephanie from her picture. She'd filled out since then—in all the right places. Her face was still narrow, but that only made her high cheekbones stand out even more. Her eyes were an odd coppery-brown; they looked almost too large for her face, like the huge staring eyes of a half-starved alley cat. The sunlight slanting in through the window picked up glints of red and gold in Stephanie's brown hair. It looked as if it had been freshly shampooed. She must have washed it because she knew we were coming, Alex thought, encouraged by this small sign that Stephanie had shown some interest in making a good impression on her new family.

One thing hadn't changed, though—Stephanie still

wasn't smiling. Alex didn't blame her much. What was there to smile about in this place?

"Out with it," Mrs. Greenspan ordered harshly, glaring at Stephanie's cigarette as she brought it defiantly to her lips. "You know the rules, young lady. No smoking in the rooms."

With a shrug, Stephanie crushed her cigarette out in the mayonnaise jar lid that sat on her dresser, beside a ratty old lamp. "Whatever you say, Mrs. G," she drawled.

Her gaze flicked over to Alex, who thought she saw the barest glimmer of amusement in Stephanie's can-you-believe-what-I-have-to-put-up-with? expression. As if she were enlisting Alex as an ally. Then it was gone, her face blank as stone once again. Alex wondered if she'd imagined it.

An awkward pause followed, and Alex took a deep breath, plunging in. "Hi! I'm Alex," she said brightly, but to her own ears her voice sounded forced, over-eager.

"Alex who?" Stephanie stared at her with those blank alley-cat eyes.

Alex's cheeks burned as if she'd been slapped. She'd expected shyness on Stephanie's part, even some resentment . . . but not this stony indifference.

"I . . . we're, uh . . ." she faltered, hating herself for losing control of the situation. ". . . You're going to be living with us."

Her mother and father stepped forth in a flurry of introductions that saved her from any further embarrassment.

"I'm Mrs. Enomoto . . . but, please, call me Susan.

15

I want you to think of us as your family," Alex's mom gushed nervously, holding tightly to the strap of her leather shoulder bag as if to a lifeline. She didn't try to hug Stephanie as Alex had thought she might. A good thing, too. Stephanie looked about as cuddly as an armadillo right now.

Dad shook her hand formally. In his deep, cultured voice, he said, "We're very, very happy you've decided to live with us, Stephanie."

"It wasn't my decision," she said in a flat, matter-of-fact voice.

Annoyance flared in Alex. Did she have to say that, even if it was the truth? How much effort did it take to at least *act* polite, even if you didn't feel it?

Then she quickly reminded herself of everything Stephanie had gone through. Miss Bryson had warned them it wouldn't be easy; they would have to be patient. Still Alex had to struggle against her rising irritation. Unfortunately, patience wasn't one of her top-ten virtues.

Gritting her teeth, Alex plunged in once again, determined not to let her good intentions be shot down so easily.

"You'll be going to school with me," she informed Stephanie enthusiastically. "Glenwood's a neat place. You'll like it. I even arranged with Mr. Rodriguez for us to be in some of the same classes. He's my counselor. He's really cool. You'll like him." She knew she was babbling but couldn't stop herself.

Why didn't Stephanie *say* something? What did it take to get her to smile? Alex had that hollow feeling in the pit of her stomach, the kind she got before a really difficult dive when she was poised at the end of the

16

board, looking down at the water. What were they getting into with this girl?

"Schools are all alike," Stephanie replied. "I've been to enough to know." She spoke in that same bored tone.

For once, Alex could think of nothing to say. It was as if she'd run smack into a brick wall. She looked over just in time to catch the uneasy glance her mom shot her dad.

"Well, I suppose we should get going," Susan said, quickly recovering her natural poise. "It's a long drive, and I thought we might stop for lunch on the way home."

Stephanie rose from the bed. She stood there, waiting for them to make the next move, her hands awkwardly stuffed into her pockets, her jaw jutting out at an angle. It was the first glimpse Alex had had of how difficult this must be for her, too.

"Do you have a suitcase?" Dad asked. Alex followed his glance as it swept about the cubicle, with its plain metal bed and dresser. The pale green walls and worn linoleum floor glared back, ugly and bare.

Alex thought guiltily of her own cozy room at home, its shelves crammed with diving trophies, the bright yellow walls splashed with colorful posters. She winced in sympathy as Stephanie fished a ratty army-green backpack from under the bed. It looked as if it had been through both world wars.

"I travel light," Stephanie spoke quickly, defensively. "Too much stuff just ties a person down." Color flared in her cheeks.

"I know what you mean," Alex jumped in to the rescue. "I've been meaning to get rid of a lot of my stuff, too. Most of it just sits around in my closet, anyway. Hey, maybe the two of us could organize a garage sale one of these days."

"Yeah . . . maybe," Stephanie said, her expression thawing slightly.

But by the time they were ready to leave, the two of them settled into the backseat of the family station wagon, with Mom and Dad in front, Stephanie had closed up again. She lit another cigarette and went back to staring out the window. Alex rolled her window down to keep from choking on the smoke.

She wished her friends were here. Kit and Elaine would be joking around, easing the tension with their sense of humor, and Lori would know just the right thing to say to put Stephanie at ease. The trouble was, Stephanie didn't act as if she were nervous. While the rest of them were a bundle of knots, she appeared perfectly cool and unconcerned.

Alex was sure it was only a facade, but how did you go about cracking through a brick wall?

Surprisingly, it was Stephanie who broke the silence. "This house of yours. Is it big? I mean, am I gonna have my own space?"

"Your own room? Sure. It's next to mine."

She tried not to let herself think of it as Noodle's room.

For the first time, Stephanie allowed herself the tiniest smile. "Not bad. The last place I stayed at, I had to share a room with this girl, Paula. Man, what a trip! All she did was talk about this guy she was in love with. I practically went nuts listening to all that garbage."

They'd passed the city limits. Orchards, pink and

green, began to replace the gray office buildings of downtown San Jose. The late morning air rushing in through the window smelled of blossoming fruit trees. But they were still a long way from Glenwood.

"I have a boyfriend," Alex confessed with a little laugh, "but I promise not to bore you with all the details."

"Yeah?" Stephanie seemed interested, despite her scornful comment about her former foster sister. "What's his name?"

"Danny. We're on the diving team together. In fact, that's sort of how we met. It's a long story." She grinned. "I'll save it for some night when we've got nothing better to talk about."

She could go on and on about Danny, but now definitely wasn't the time, even though it was the first thing they'd talked about that Stephanie seemed interested in.

"I'll bet he's a real Tarzan, huh?" Stephanie's smile widened slightly.

Alex couldn't tell if Stephanie was serious or not, but she decided to play along as if it were all a joke.

"Sure. That's us. Tarzan and Jane. Except I don't let Danny boss me around. Mostly, he says its the other way around. I guess I *do* get a little bossy sometimes, but we're really crazy about each other." She laughed. "Or maybe we're just crazy, period."

Stephanie turned back to the window. "I've never felt that way about a guy," she said in a soft, almost regretful voice. "Most of the ones I've known were too stuck on themselves to care about anyone else."

"Wait till you meet Danny. He's not like that. You'll see." Alex knew she was bragging, but she couldn't help it. Danny was the only one around who didn't seem to realize what a hunk he was.

"I can't wait." Again, Alex wasn't sure if she was being sincere or sarcastic. With Stephanie, it was hard to tell.

Alex wasn't the type to give up easily, though. She took a deep breath. "You know, we really *are* glad you'll be living with us," she said in a rush. "I know it must be hard for you, getting used to a new family and all. But honestly, we're not so bad once you get to know us."

Stephanie was silent, staring out the window, smoking. When she finally turned to look at Alex, one corner of her mouth was twisted up in a funny expression that was more a sneer than a smile.

"That family I was living with before—you know, the one I was telling you about? Well, this girl, Paula, she got knocked up. Her parents blamed me for it. They said I was a 'bad influence.' And I didn't even have a boyfriend. What a laugh, huh?"

Alex didn't think it was very funny; it sounded unfair . . . and sad. That was what she found hardest to understand about Stephanie, how she could talk as if her feelings didn't matter at all.

"Is that why you ran away?" Alex asked softly.

"I *told* you about that. I just don't like being tied down." She looked angry.

"But if they'd been nicer to you . . ."

Stephanie's eyes narrowed as she drew on her cigarette. She exhaled in a hard, angry puff. "Man, you don't know *anything*."

Alex sank back in her seat, stung into silence. She had a sick feeling in her stomach—the kind of feeling she sometimes got during a dive, before she even hit the water, when she knew she was going to land wrong, and it was too late to do anything about it.

This was going to be a lot harder than she'd imagined, even in her worst thoughts. Maybe her biggest challenge yet.

# CHAPTER THREE

"This is your room," Alex told Stephanie, the words snagging in her throat. She ached with the effort of not saying "my brother's room."

Alex followed Stephanie's gaze as she took in the freshly painted room, with its pretty lace curtains and brand-new flowered bedspread. Gone was that funny old wallpaper Dad had put up before Noodle was born, and then hadn't had the heart to take down—little football players sprinting across a backdrop of blue. The chessboard and card table by the window had been packed away, along with all the books, papers, and old crossword puzzles that had overflowed from the bookcase in the corner. Next to the bed, where

Noodle's respirator had always stood, sat a newly re-finished antique pine dresser on which Mom had thoughtfully arranged a vase of fresh flowers.

"Looks like nobody ever lived in it," Stephanie commented, dropping her backpack on the rocking chair by the door. "Like a picture in one of those house magazines."

Alex thought so, too. She wished her mother hadn't erased every trace of Noodle, but she understood her reasons—Mom hadn't wanted all those constant re-minders around.

"This was my brother's room."

Stephanie shifted uncomfortably. "Oh, yeah. Miss Bryson told me. He died, right?"

Alex gave a quick nod.

"Oh." Stephanie sat down on the bed. "I never knew anyone who died. Unless maybe my mother died with-out me knowing about it. I haven't seen her since I was five." Then, as if afraid she'd revealed too much, she jumped up and paced over to the window, which looked out over the backyard. "Who's that guy mowing the lawn? Is he your uncle or something?"

"No. That's Miguel. He's our gardener."

Stephanie swung around. She looked genuinely impressed. "You must be pretty loaded. I mean, your old man being a doctor and all. This place is some-thing else."

Alex was embarrassed. Who did Stephanie think they were—the Rockefellers? "We're not really that rich. A lot of people around here have bigger houses than we do." But she could see it was useless to try and convince Stephanie. Compared to what she was used

24

to, they probably did seem rich beyond belief.

Alex went over to the closet. "You can put your things away in here if you like." She paused, remembering the raggedy backpack. Casually, she added, "Oh, and don't worry about clothes for school or anything. I've got plenty of stuff you can borrow. You look like you're about the same size as me."

"Who's worried?" Stephanie said, that defensive edge creeping into her voice. "I have everything I need."

"I didn't mean . . ." Alex shrugged. It was no use. Stephanie wouldn't believe she was only trying to be nice. Talking to her was like picking your way through a minefield.

Pushed to the back of the closet was a cardboard box full of things that had belonged to Noodle, which Mom probably hadn't had the heart to throw away when she cleared out the room. Alex picked out the trophy that lay on top of a pile of clothes. The tender spot in her throat began to throb.

"He won this last year at the junior state chess championship." She spoke softly, hugging the trophy to her chest. "You should have seen him play. I could never beat him, not when he was really trying. He was the best . . . the best at everything." With the edge of her sweat shirt, she lovingly wiped away the dust that had collected along the bottom of the trophy. "That's how he got his nickname—Noodle. Dad would always say, 'That's using your noodle,' and after a while it just stuck. His real name was Jimmy, only everybody just called him Noodle . . ."

Alex stopped, brushing a tear from her eye. She

25

didn't want Stephanie to see her crying. Quickly, she stuffed the trophy back in the box and shut the closet door.

"I talk too much," she said, forcing a little laugh. "That's one thing about me you've probably noticed. Once I get started, you can't shut me up."

Stephanie shrugged. "Don't sweat it." A reluctant smile stole over her pretty, dark features. "After Paula, nobody can faze me."

The phone rang out in the hallway.

"That's probably Danny," Alex said. "He said he'd call. Listen . . . if you want to take a shower or anything, well, you know where everything is. Just, uh, make yourself at home."

"Don't worry about me. I can take care of myself."

Alex dashed out into the hallway, feeling relieved to get away from Stephanie. The tension between them crackled in the air like static electricity.

But it wasn't Danny calling. It was one of her mother's friends, and Alex was disappointed. There was so much she wanted to tell Danny about Stephanie.

When she returned to Stephanie's room, Stephanie had put away her belongings and was fiddling with the dial on the radio that had been Noodle's. A flash of gold on the windowsill caught Alex's eye. Noodle's trophy! How had it gotten there? She remembered putting it back in the closet.

Alex cast a questioning glance at Stephanie, who shrugged, looking embarrassed.

"I figured since it was your brother's room and all, you wouldn't want all his stuff sitting in the closet," she said.

Alex was taken aback by this unexpected touch of thoughtfulness, which she never would have expected from Stephanie. Was she really as tough as she wanted them to think?

"That was really nice of you," Alex said. "I mean, it's still your room. Noodle would have wanted it that way. But thanks for understanding."

Stephanie frowned, her cheeks growing red. "Look, I wasn't trying to win points," she said sharply. "Let's get one thing straight, okay? I go my way, you go yours. I don't do anybody any favors, and I don't expect anybody to do favors for me. Got it?"

Alex felt her own quick temper flare. "Some people happen to *like* doing favors!" she cried. "It wouldn't kill you to let somebody be nice to you once in a while!"

"Look, I know the scene. You want to be nice to me so you can feel like you've done your bit for the homeless kids of the world." Stephanie avoided her eyes. She picked up a magazine that lay on the nightstand, then tossed it down without looking at it.

Alex stared at her, realization sinking in. "You don't want to like us, do you? Are you afraid we'll be like your last foster family—blaming you for everything? Is that it? Come on, at least give us a chance!"

She could see she'd touched a nerve. Stephanie went rigid, her coppery eyes flaring with emotion. "I didn't ask to be here." She turned her back on Alex with a hard, angry movement.

Alex went over and touched her shoulder. "Look, I know things haven't been so easy for you up till now. I was just trying to . . ."

Stephanie jerked around to face her. "I *know* what you're trying to do. You think I haven't seen it before?

27

All you people who act like not having parents is one of those diseases you donate money for. Well, I don't want your charity. I'm sick of being somebody's pet cause!"

"Nobody thinks of you that way."

"Oh yeah?" Stephanie paused, her faced flushed. "Tell me, then—what's in it for you? What are you and your parents getting out of all this?"

Alex blurted the first thing that came to mind. "We thought you'd want to live with us!"

"Well you thought *wrong*. I don't need anybody." Stephanie went back to fiddling with the radio. She found a station blaring harsh rock music and turned it up full blast, drowning out any further attempts at conversation.

Alex spun away in frustration. Sure, she felt sorry for Stephanie, but not *that* kind of sorry. Only there was nothing she could say, nothing she could do to convince Stephanie of that. When she tried to be nice, that only seemed to make things worse.

The house that had seemed so huge and empty since Noodle had died suddenly felt small and cramped. Stephanie had been living with them for less than a day, and already Alex couldn't wait to get away.

She decided she wouldn't wait for Danny to call her. She'd call him. Better yet, she'd go over and see him. Right now what she needed most was to feel Danny's reassuring arms about her.

"I'm sorry, Danny. I can't. I . . . I guess I'm just not in the mood." Alex wound her arms around his neck

28

and squeezed him tightly, letting him know she still loved him anyway.

They lay scrunched together on top of his twin bed. Danny stopped kissing her and rolled over onto his back. Alex hugged herself, feeling cold all of a sudden. She'd taken her sweat shirt off, but she was still wearing her bra and jeans. Danny hadn't undressed either, but she could see from the red, frustrated look on his face that he wished he could.

She looked away, staring out the window. It was getting dark. How had it gotten so late without her realizing it? Time had a way of slipping by up in Danny's room . . . especially when his parents weren't around.

She loved it up here. Danny's room was way up in the attic, with a window that opened out onto the branches of a huge acacia tree. The room was so small it was like being in a tree house.

She looked back at Danny. He was quiet, staring up at the ceiling—too quiet, except for the funny way he was breathing. "I'm really sorry. Do you mind if we don't this time?"

"No, it's okay." He was silent for a moment, then asked, "Are you worried my parents are going to come back? I told you, they won't be back until tonight. They never get back early from auctions. Mom likes to stay until the last. She's sure she'll win a five-dollar bid on a box of junk one of these days that'll turn out to be a set of Paul Revere silverware or something."

"It's not that." But even as she said it, Alex had a sudden image of Danny's parents bursting into the room like a SWAT team—Danny's balding stockbroker

29

father and his pleasant mother who ran an antique shop. She giggled. "Do you think they *know?*"

Alex and Danny had been going steady since last year, but had only become really intimate a short while ago. They tried to be careful, but it was hard to find places where they could be alone, so they sometimes took chances. His attic room was a favorite spot, but they always worried they would be discovered.

"I think my mother suspects," Danny said. "Last week when I told her I thought it was time I graduated to a double bed, she gave me this really funny look."

"You *didn't.*" Alex pretended to be shocked. "You didn't really ask for a double bed?"

Danny grinned. "You're the one who's always saying this bed isn't big enough for both of us."

"You didn't tell your mom that, did you?"

"Do you think I'm crazy?"

Alex leaned over and kissed the tip of his sunburned nose. "Yes. It's one of the reasons I love you."

"I told her it was for Einstein." Einstein was Danny's German shepherd, who lived up to his name as far as smartness was concerned. He thought he was a person, and since people don't sleep on the floor, he had a habit of climbing onto Danny's bed in the middle of the night. "He needs a lot of room to spread out."

Alex laughed. "I'm not sure I like the idea of you using your dog as an excuse to sleep with me. Though it *would* be nice if you had a bigger bed."

"I wish we had one right now." He sighed wistfully, tucking his hands behind his head.

"I told you," Alex said, her laughter fading. "It's got nothing to do with you, or your parents, or this bed.

30

I'm just uptight. This thing with Stephanie, I guess it's got me more upset than I realized."

She'd poured out the whole story when she first arrived at his house. Upset and disappointed, she'd even started to cry a little. Danny had put his arms around her, consoling her with a kiss. One thing had led to another and . . . well, here they were.

"Maybe it's not as bad as you think," Danny said. "It's possible you might be making this into a bigger problem than it is really going to be."

Alex felt a surge of annoyance. How could he say such a thing? What did he know about it? It almost sounded as if he were accusing her. As if it were *her* fault things had gotten off to a bad start with Stephanie. What she'd wanted from Danny was reassurance and support, and instead he was putting the blame onto her!

She stared at him. His polo shirt had come untucked from his Levi's; it was pushed up under his arms, revealing the hard brown square of his stomach. He was only wearing one sock—the other one lay crumpled on the bedspread. He looked so adorably sexy, her annoyance faded in spite of herself.

At moments like this, she could hardly believe he was hers. He was so handsome and popular . . . and really sweet, besides—not stuck-up about his looks the way some of the popular boys at Glenwood were.

He could have anyone, she thought. Alex had seen the notes girls slipped into his locker. She'd been at his house when they called, pretending to want some homework assignment as an excuse to talk to him. He always laughed it off, but sometimes she couldn't help

31

feeling jealous. Especially after they'd had a fight, when she found herself wondering what had made Danny choose *her*.

Sure, they had a lot in common. They both loved outdoors stuff, though Danny wasn't as competitive as she was in sports. They liked the same kind of movies and shared a passion for Mexican food and Häagen-Dazs chocolate chocolate-chip ice cream, hanging out at the beach, and watching videos. But those were just surface interests. Underneath, they were as different as night and day.

Danny didn't understand her moods, for one thing. Oh, he was sympathetic when something was bothering her, but she often felt he wasn't really on her side. Maybe it was because they approached difficult situations with such different attitudes. Alex liked to meet them head-on. Danny's philosophy was to leave them alone and hope they would work themselves out.

At the moment, Alex felt as if a line had been drawn down the middle of the bed, putting her on one side and Danny on the other, when all she'd wanted was to be comforted and held.

"I'm *not* making a big thing out of this." She propped herself up on one elbow so that she was gazing down at him, her hair sliding against his cheek. "How can you say a thing like that when you weren't even there?"

"Hey, c'mon, Alex. I didn't mean it in a bad way." He rubbed her shoulder. "I just meant . . . well, you know how you get sometimes."

Alex frowned. That really got to her—Danny assuming that when something went wrong it just naturally had to be because of the way she was . . . not just because of the situation.

"No," she glared. "I *don't* know."

Danny withdrew his hand. "What I meant was—you expect too much from other people sometimes. I guess you can't help it, though. It's just the way you are."

"You make it sound like some kind of awful sickness!"

"Come off it, Alex." Danny was beginning to sound annoyed, too. "You're twisting around everything I say, making it worse."

Panic overrode her annoyance. Was this turning into another one of their fights? Oh, God, she hoped not. They'd been fighting too much lately.

Last weekend it was a dumb argument they'd had over the phone. Danny had wanted to skip diving practice to go surfing with his friends. Alex had told him he was blowing it as far as the team and Coach Reeves were concerned. Then Danny had said something like, if Coach Reeves kicked him off the team, he'd probably be doing him a big favor. Alex had been so furious with his attitude, she'd hung up.

The really awful part was, she didn't even know why they fought so much. What was happening to them? They'd been so close before; they still were, but now it always seemed as if they were tugging at each other, pulling in opposite directions, without either of them wanting to let go.

"What's that got to do with Stephanie?" she asked, veering away from her own problems with Danny, which were scarier to face in some ways than the one she had with Stephanie.

33

"I don't know. Maybe nothing. I was only wondering if you were expecting too much, too soon. Give the poor kid a chance. She's been bounced around so much, she probably feels like a Ping-Pong ball. Maybe she just needs some time to settle in before she can open up."

"I *know* what she's been through. I'm trying to be understanding. But you didn't see the way she was acting. She practically bit my head off every time I got near her. I was only trying to be nice!"

"Maybe you're being too nice," he said.

"What's wrong with being too nice?"

"You want her to feel like a member of the family, right?"

"Right."

"Well, if she was really your sister, would you let her get away with acting like that? Wouldn't you tell her just to shove it?"

"I guess so. But she's not my sister."

"You see? That's just the point. You spent ten minutes telling me how you wanted her to feel like a member of the family. But you're being so nice to her, it's making her feel more like an outsider than ever."

"How come you know so much?"

"I don't. I just happen to know what it's like being around you." He grinned. "Like being in the middle of a hurricane."

She socked his arm. "Thanks a lot."

He caught her to him, pulling her against his chest. She could feel his warm breath tickling the roots of her hair. "I'm not complaining. I love you, Alex. But you *do* come on pretty strong sometimes."

34

"Look who's talking." He couldn't hide the fact that he still wanted her.

"It's your fault for being so sexy," he murmured. "How do you expect me to keep my hands off you when you're lying next to me practically naked?"

"I am *not* naked!"

He fumbled at her back, and she felt the elastic of her bra give. "You will be soon if you plan on staying on this bed much longer."

Alex grew very still. She hadn't stopped feeling angry at him, and she wanted him to know it. But even though she was still mad, she couldn't ignore the ripples of excitement that spread through her as his warm fingers danced lightly over her back. Her body was such a traitor!

Danny sensed her withdrawal. His hand stopped moving. "I was just kidding," he said softly, the playfulness gone from his voice. "If you're not in the mood . . ."

Alex relented, touched by his thoughtfulness. A lot of boys would've just forged right ahead. At least Danny had cared enough not to force her into anything she didn't want to do.

She touched his cheek. "I'm in the mood now." It was true in one sense. Her body was in the mood, even if her mind wasn't.

"Did you bring It?" he asked. *It*, meaning her diaphragm.

Alex nodded, smiling as his kisses traveled in a butterfly path up her neck.

Deep down in her heart, though, she still hadn't forgiven him completely for being so ready to find fault in the way she was dealing with Stephanie, even though what he'd said was probably true. That only made it harder to swallow.

The trouble was, when Danny was kissing her, she had a habit of forgetting everything else. His mouth played over hers, gently, warming her to the soles of her feet. His hand slid down the curve of her spine, sending a shudder of delight through her.

She surrendered to the good feelings with a sigh, wishing they could have had their argument someplace other than bed. It was impossible to stay mad at Danny when he was making love to her.

# CHAPTER FOUR

"Do you always knock yourself out like that?" a voice called over from the bleachers as Alex was climbing out of the school pool following her lunchtime laps.

Alex squinted in the bright sunlight, pushing up the goggles she wore to keep the chlorine out of her eyes. A lone figure sat hunched over her knees on the bottom riser—a girl in jeans and a familiar denim jacket, her dark brown hair blowing in the breeze.

What was Stephanie doing here? She'd rejected Alex's earlier attempt to play tour guide. Even though it was only her first day at Glenwood, she said she'd prefer to check out the campus on her own. It was obvious she wanted no part of Alex's social life, or even Alex herself.

Alex grabbed the towel she'd left by the ladder and walked over. "I only have half an hour, so if I want to get in thirty laps, I have to hustle," she explained.

"How come you have to practice at lunchtime?"

Alex laughed. "I don't *have* to. I want to. It's the only time the pool's empty, except for super-early in the morning. The truth is I'm really lazy at heart. I hate getting up at the crack of dawn." Lightly, she asked, "What brings you here?"

Stephanie shrugged. "I happened to be around, that's all." She wore that remote, guarded expression Alex was beginning to know so well. The look that said, loud and clear, *No Trespassing.* "Anyway, there's not much going on around here. Glenwood's a pretty dull place."

Dull! How could Stephanie make such a snap judgment based on one morning's observation? All she had to do was look a little bit past her own nose, and she'd see that there was a lot going on. Right now Alex could think of at least half a dozen activities that would be interesting and fun.

The noon movie sponsored by the Glee Club was by far the most popular lunch hour event. Today they were showing the first half hour installment of *Star Wars.* Half the school would be crowded into the gym to watch. It was always a lot of fun, like one big party, with a lot of booing and cheering and stomping feet, and kids ad-libbing funny lines during the scenes that were supposed to be serious. Alex would've gone herself if she hadn't seen *Star Wars* at least ten times already.

Maybe that was Stephanie's excuse as well. But there must be *something* about Glenwood she'd found interesting.

"What did you think of Mr. Janovick?" Alex asked. She was sure Stephanie must have at least appreciated the English class Alex had gotten her into. "It's a good class, isn't it? He's the best teacher at Glenwood."

Alex had had to practically move mountains to get Stephanie in, too. Everybody wanted to be in Mr. J's class, and there were always a dozen more kids trying to get transferred in than he had room for. Mostly, it was because Mr. J really loved teaching, and it showed. Right now they were in the midst of translating *Hamlet* into modern-day slang, which was turning out to be a riot.

"It was okay," Stephanie said. "But we already did *Hamlet* at my last school."

"Not like this, I'll bet." Alex grinned, remembering the line Anita Fuller had made up. In place of, "To be, or not to be . . . ," she had substituted, "Hey, things are coming down pretty heavy around here—maybe I oughta think about checking out."

"I think it's pretty dumb, if you ask me. What's the point of learning *Hamlet*, unless it's the way Shakespeare wrote it?"

"Mr. J's point is, you can't really learn something unless you understand it," Alex argued. "A lot of those kids might just as well be reading *Hamlet* in Greek. This way, they'll really know what it's all about."

"If you say so." Stephanie looked away, obviously bored with the whole discussion.

Alex frowned in annoyance. She hadn't expected

Stephanie to thank her, but couldn't she have shown a little bit of enthusiasm? Alex draped her towel around her neck and started to walk off.

"Where are you going?" Stephanie asked.

"The locker room. I don't want to hold you up," Alex said, coolly. "I'm sure you have a lot of sightseeing to do."

"I'm not doing anything special. I think I'll just hang out here for a while."

Alex hesitated. She was fed up with the way Stephanie had been acting, but that didn't mean she should give up on her completely. Besides, Stephanie had really sounded lonely just now. It made Alex sad to think of her sitting out here all alone on her first day of school. She didn't believe Stephanie could really prefer it that way.

She turned around, relenting. "Listen, I'll only be a couple of minutes. Then I'm heading up to the gym to meet my friends. Why don't you come with me? I'd like you to meet them."

Stephanie didn't answer right away. She remained staring off into the distance, as if thinking over whether or not she wanted to be bothered. Alex was on the verge of telling her to forget the whole thing when finally she replied, "Yeah, okay. Might as well. I've got nothing better to do."

The movie was still on when they arrived. Alex and Stephanie didn't have to buy tickets, though, since the reel was almost over. Alex picked her way across the darkened gym toward the rows of folding chairs lined up in front of the movie screen.

The chairs were packed, and there were kids seated on the floor as well. Alex and Stephanie had to step over more than one pair of legs, as they searched for an empty place to sit down. Until the lights came on, she could forget about finding her friends, so she might just as well enjoy what was left of the movie.

Up on the screen Luke Skywalker battled it out with a band of aliens. "Sock it to 'em, Luke!" somebody yelled. The music soared to a spine-tingling climax. Dum-da-*da*-dum. It always hit Alex right in the pit of her stomach. She loved exciting movies—movies with nonstop action and fearless heroes and heroines. Her friends had even told her she reminded them of Princess Leia. She wished real life were more like that— instant, dramatic solutions for every problem. If her life at this very moment were a movie, she'd include a scene where she introduced Stephanie to Kit, Elaine, and Lori, and they all hit it off instantly.

But life wasn't the movies, was it?

"Alex . . . over here!" a voice hissed at her.

Alex peered around. A slender arm waving at her from the middle row caught her attention. Even in the dim light, she recognized Elaine's shiny brown hair and amber eyes. She was sitting with her boyfriend, Carl. Elaine gestured toward the chair next to Carl, which she'd saved by stacking her binder and a pile of books on.

Alex motioned for Stephanie to follow her as she squeezed past a row of knees to where Elaine and Carl were sitting. Carl stood up when he saw Stephanie.

"You can have my chair," he whispered. "I have to leave anyway. I get faint at the sight of robots being disemboweled." With an impish grin, he leaned down and kissed Elaine. "Bye, catch you later."

Watching him dart off, Alex couldn't help mentally

comparing him to the White Rabbit in Alice in Wonderland. He was always looking at his watch and rushing off somewhere. But Elaine didn't seem to mind; she was used to it by now. They'd been going together since January.

"Carl has to study for a test," Elaine explained in a low voice as Alex wedged into the seat beside her, with Stephanie on her other side.

Alex wasn't surprised. Carl was always studying for something or other. Same with Elaine. They were both in the Honors program, which was only open to straight-A students. Even though they fought sometimes, they were more alike than they realized. Unlike her and Danny . . .

Alex's thoughts were interrupted when Elaine whispered in her ear. "I figured you might finish with practice early—that's why I saved you a seat. If I'd known you were bringing Stephanie, I would have saved two." Her amber eyes shone with curiosity. She leaned closer. "That's *her*, isn't it?"

Alex was on the verge of introducing Elaine to Stephanie when suddenly the movie screen went blank, and the sound groaned to a halt.

A chorus of grumbles broke out.

"What happened?" a boy yelled. "Time's not up yet!"

"The film must've broke!" another voice clamored.

The lights came on in a blaze. Alex blinked in the sudden glare, her vision focusing on the girl who had appeared out of nowhere, positioning herself in front of the screen. She looked slightly out of breath, and her blond curls fluttered untidily about her heart-shaped face. In her short red skirt, she had no trouble getting the audience's attention, or at least the male portion of it. The grumbles immediately turned to appreciative wolf whistles.

Alex smiled, nudging Elaine with her elbow and whispering, "That's Kit for you. She could probably take their mind off anything, even a nuclear blast."

The trouble was, Kit never anticipated the effect she inevitably produced, and was always a little embarrassed by it. Alex watched her cheeks go from pink to bright red. She brought a hand to her head, nervously raking her fingers through her curls. Her wide blue eyes held a trapped look, but she didn't back down.

"Listen up, you guys!" Kit shouted, ignoring the whistles and catcalls as best she could. "We're having a little trouble with the projector. Don't panic. It'll be fixed by tomorrow." More groans and grumbles. "Okay, I know how you feel. I'm not happy about it, either. But the reel was almost over anyhow."

"Do we get our money back?" a boy in the front row called out.

"Don't forget—it's for a good cause," Kit shot back. She grinned. "Maybe we'll even use the money to buy a new projector."

Some people laughed. Kit's small joke had made them forget their annoyance. There was even a smattering of applause as she stepped down. Then everyone began shuffling around, unearthing books and backpacks from under chairs, calling out to one another, banging open doors. The noise was overwhelming.

Outside, Kit came running over to join her friends as they were walking toward the benches that lined the brick quad.

"Wow, I wasn't sure I was going to get out of there

alive!" she announced breathlessly. "Now I know how General Custer must've felt facing all those Indians. Maybe we should start showing boring movies, so no one will complain if the projector breaks down." She glanced over at Stephanie, her enormous blue eyes lighting up with friendliness. "Oh, hi. You must be Stephanie. I'm Kit. I've heard a lot about you."

Stephanie nodded briefly in acknowledgment. "Yeah, I can imagine," she said with a tight little laugh.

Kit blushed. She hadn't meant it *that* way, Alex knew. Stephanie seemed to always imagine the very worst in what people said or did.

Elaine stuck out her hand. "I'm Elaine. I just hope Alex hasn't told you too much about *us*. We've done some pretty looney things together. When we were all in the sixth grade Alex named us the Three Nutsketeers. That was before Lori joined the group." She giggled. "Now we're the Fearless Four. We'll have to think up a new name now that you're here."

"Where *is* Lori?" Alex asked.

"Three guesses," Kit said.

Alex laughed. "I only need one. She's with Perry, right?"

"He said he had something important he wanted to talk to her about. They're eating lunch up in the Grove." Kit gave a knowing smile. "But I don't think either of them had food on their mind. I wonder what made his news so earth-shattering that it was worth missing *Star Wars*?"

"Maybe he heard from that college in Kalamazoo," Elaine suggested. "Lori is sort of upset about it. She was hoping they wouldn't be living too far apart next year." Lori had hopes of becoming a model in New York after graduation; she was compiling her portfolio to send to a list of agents Kit's older cousin had gotten for her.

Alex noticed Elaine was wearing one of her pre-makeover outfits—tan slacks and a dark green blouse, which was saved from drabness by a pretty striped scarf. She supposed old habits were hard to break, though thankfully Elaine hadn't slipped back into wearing glasses since she'd gotten her contact lenses.

"Where's Kalamazoo?" Kit asked. "Isn't that somewhere in Africa?"

"It's in Michigan, silly." Elaine laughed.

The four of them drifted over toward the benches. Alex found one that was partially in the shade, under the branches of the huge eucalyptus tree that sheltered a corner of the quad. Its burly trunk, scarred with hearts and initials, was a living record of the romances at Glenwood High, both past and present.

Alex fingered the initials Danny had carved there once upon a time—"D.R. and A.E. Forever." Corny, but she'd loved it anyway. She thought about how it would always be there, even long after they had left the school. Suddenly, she felt a flicker of sadness, reminded of how she and Danny seemed to be drifting apart lately. Was there really such a thing as forever?

Her attention was jolted back to Stephanie, who had pulled a cigarette from the front pocket of her denim jacket and was lighting it.

"We're not allowed to smoke on campus," Alex told her. "They're really pretty strict about it, too."

Stephanie shrugged. "What's the big deal? I'm not hurting anyone, am I?"

45

Both Kit and Elaine exchanged anxious, embarrassed looks. Kit spoke up. "You're right, Stephanie. It's no big deal for one person. It's just that if *everybody* did it, there would be a problem." She obviously didn't want to make a big deal out of it for Alex's sake. "Anyway, why ask for trouble? If you get in hot water with the office on your first day, they'll be hounding you for the rest of the year."

Ignoring Kit's advice, Stephanie took a long pull on her cigarette. "Yeah, well, I'm used to trouble. I don't let it bother me too much."

Alex's heart sank. Oh, God, this wasn't turning out at all the way she'd hoped. Stephanie was showing her very worst side to her friends. What were they going to think?

She tried to laugh it off. "We've all been in trouble before." Alex turned to Elaine. "Remember that double date when we stayed out past curfew, and you didn't want to wake your parents up when you realized you'd forgotten your key?"

Elaine groaned. "Do I ever! Of all the bright ideas I've had in my life, the brightest was *not* sneaking in through the window."

"She tried to stand on Carl's shoulders, and they both collapsed into the bushes," Alex explained.

"We made so much noise, the neighbors called the police," Elaine said. "Boy, talk about trouble! I had a lot of explaining to do that time. Then Andy—she's my younger sister—she made this big thing about me being in the bushes with Carl, and why didn't we fool around in the backseat of the car like everybody else? I could've killed her!"

"I got picked up by the police once," Stephanie said

46

quietly, almost as if she were talking to herself. She squinted against the smoke that drifted up into her eyes, her expression distant. "They kept me in jail for the whole weekend. My foster parents figured it would be the best punishment. They thought it would really teach me a lesson." She snorted. "It did. This other kid who was in with me told me how she hot-wired cars. Man, you really learn a lot in Juvy."

Alex was stunned. Miss Bryson hadn't mentioned anything about Stephanie having a police record! Or maybe she'd told Mom and Dad, and just not her.

"What did you get arrested for?" she asked.

Stephanie shrugged. "Nothing much. I got caught shoplifting. A lousy pack of smokes. You'd have thought I was trying to rob a bank the way they acted."

A prickle of apprehension raced up the back of Alex's neck. Stephanie's attitudes were so alien to her. How would they ever be able to understand each other? Alex couldn't imagine shoplifting, for instance. She knew plenty of kids who did it, just for the thrill of seeing if they could get away with it. It was a game—a dangerous and stupid one, in Alex's opinion.

Stephanie caught her look and laughed. "Don't look so nervous. I'm not going to steal anything of yours, if that's what you're worried about. I don't plan on making a career out of it."

"It's not *me* I'm worried about," Alex said pointedly.

A group of boys walked past just then. Several heads turned back for a second look at their bench. They were staring straight at Stephanie. New girls always got the once-over, Alex recalled. It was a kind of initiation rite. And she could see from the expressions on those boys' faces that Stephanie had passed with flying colors. Despite the fact that she wore no makeup and her clothes did nothing to emphasize her femininity, Stephanie was undeniably pretty.

The bell rang, signaling the end of lunch period. Elaine grabbed her books. Kit slung her backpack over one shoulder. Alex looked at Stephanie, who sat smoking her cigarette as if she had all the time in the world.

"I'll show you where your chemistry class is, but we'll have to hurry," she offered impatiently. "I've got Spanish, and its way over on the other side of the campus."

"No sweat, I can find it myself." Stephanie rose, brushing a fleck of ash from her faded jeans.

Alex was so angry, she hardly trusted herself to speak. "Suit yourself," she muttered, turning away. As an afterthought, she added, "Danny's taking me home after school. You can ride with us if you want."

She'd made the offer more for her parents' sake than Stephanie's. They had asked her to make sure Stephanie got home okay. They were both worried she might run away again.

"Just don't wait around if you don't see me," Stephanie said. "I may have other plans."

Then she strolled off, while Kit and Elaine stood there gaping in astonishment.

"Is she always that way?" Kit asked. "It doesn't seem as if she's all that red hot about making new friends."

"She's not," Alex said. "And I think I'm at the top of her list of people *not* to make friends with."

"Maybe she just needs some time to warm up to you," Kit suggested hopefully. Generous Kit was al-

48

ways the first to give someone the benefit of the doubt, usually more than once.

Elaine couldn't hide her dismay. "Why didn't you *tell* us, Alex? When I called last night, you acted as if everything was okay!"

"I couldn't talk then," Alex told her. "My parents were in the room."

"What do they think of Stephanie?"

Alex sighed, tucking a loose wisp of hair under the terry sweatband about her forehead. "None of us has had much luck cracking through to her, if you want to know the truth. She acts like we're all out to get her."

"It looks to me as though it's the other way around," Kit commented.

As they cut across the lawn in the direction of their classes, Alex relaxed slightly. It was good being able to confide in her friends, and having them understand how she felt.

"Maybe you should send her over to my house," Elaine suggested. "By the time Andy and the twins got through with her, you wouldn't recognize her." She paused. "On second thought, don't. I have enough to handle with just them. Hey"—Alex felt a firm hand grasp her elbow—"you walked right through that sprinkler!"

Alex glanced down at her drawstring pants. They were soaking wet from the knees down. She'd been so caught up in her worries, she hadn't seen the sprinkler.

Kit shot her a concerned look. "Are you okay?"

Alex gave a chagrined laugh. "Just a little wet. Nothing I can't handle."

49

"I meant . . . about Stephanie." Kit lowered her voice. "I just want you to know, you can count on me if you need help."

"Me, too," Elaine chimed in.

"Help!" Alex cried, rolling her eyes.

Their laughter helped ease the tension that had been building up inside Alex ever since Stephanie's arrival. She was sorry she hadn't gone to them sooner. She only wished they could help her find some solution to the problem with her foster sister.

Suddenly, a new thought occurred to her.

"Maybe it's a man's job," Alex said.

"What do you mean?" Kit asked.

"I don't know . . . I was just thinking. If she met some boy she really liked, maybe he could get her to change her mind about hating the whole human race."

Kit grinned. "Any likely prospects in mind?"

"Not offhand. But give me time. It'd have to be a boy who was attracted to the hard-to-get type. I don't think Stephanie's the kind who faints at the sight of a gorgeous guy."

"I think you're right," Elaine observed.

Kit looked up with a bright expression. "What about Chuck Hadley? He *hates* girls who chase after him. Remember last year when Valerie Taylor baked chocolate chip cookies and left them on his desk? I'd never seen such a panic-stricken look on anyone's face in my life. You would have thought she'd gone after him with a lasso!"

Kit had given Alex a very good idea. "Chuck's in the Sierra Club with Danny and me. In fact, I saw his name on the sign-up sheet for the next overnight camping trip. Maybe if I could talk Stephanie into going, too . . ."

Kit paused, closing her eyes. "I can just picture it. They're lying outside next to the fire in their sleeping bags. The stars are shining overhead. They're so close, they just can't stand it. Chuck reaches for the zipper on her sleeping bag . . ."

"Aren't you forgetting something?" Alex interrupted.

"What?"

"Oh, nothing much. Just a chaperone, and about twenty other kids."

Kit giggled. "Well, it was just a fantasy anyway. Do you think they would really hit it off?"

"It's worth a try," Elaine said optimistically. She glanced at her watch. "Uh-oh. Gotta run. We'll have to work out the details after school."

"I have to go, too," Kit said. She stopped in front of the library. "I've got study hall this period. Ms. Poole." She made a face. "She's strict about talking, so I guess I'll really have to study."

"Don't worry, it won't kill you." Alex veered off in the direction of her Spanish class. "See you later!" she called over her shoulder as she rounded the corner.

All the way up to the language building, Alex thought about Stephanie. The more she thought about the plan, the more she decided she was on to something that could possibly turn out to be the answer to everything. The right boy just might be the key to unlocking Stephanie.

crushing me. Maybe I'd come talk. Stephanie, I'm
evil, too."

Richard had closed her eyes. "I can feel the small
place in my system—somewhere in that sleeping
bag. There are ants crawling over me." They were now
quite close to each other. "Can't I rub it for the part
on her nose?"

"Aren't you forgetting something?" Terry showed
fatigue.

"What?"

"Cullberg and the rest of it. Dignity, etc. and about
twenty other things."

"Richard." Well it was just a number anyway. Do
you think I'm weird I really care to protect

It wasn't her business and unfortunately, she
didn't let herself. "The EPA. Other than will he ever
work on another public affair school."

"I've got to face that," said Richard gently. "I feel
the breach." I tried and it all up, pushed me right—

She made a face. "She's already about enough, it was
threatened up to study.

"Don't worry. It don't fall into every corner of all," Un
stared at her Stephanie face, was not quite sur-
ronded over her anguish at the number, she smiled.

All that seemed to be the marriage building. Face
thought about everything. For more than thought
about the past. She didn't really doubt she meant to
something that all possibly important to be the ex-
posed overriding. He replies what he had inherited
to unlocks beginning.

# CHAPTER FIVE

Alex daydreamed her way through Spanish, which wasn't hard to do. Mrs. Ortega was out with the flu, and the substitute teacher was obviously the lazy type—he simply ran a film about Mexico that they'd all seen before. The only interesting part was the bullfighting scene, but even that didn't seem as dramatic to Alex as it had the first time she'd seen it. She had too many dramas going on in her own head at the moment.

After the bell, she waited outside the classroom for Lori. Lori also had Spanish fifth period with Senor Castaneda, and her class was only two doors down. Usually, Lori was waiting for her by the time she got out, but today she was nowhere in sight. Alex wondered if maybe her class had been kept late.

Then she spotted a couple of people she knew were in the course too and realized that couldn't be why Lori hadn't showed. So where was she? Lori was far too thoughtful to simply have gone ahead without telling her. Maybe she wasn't feeling well and had left class early.

Alex searched the crowd milling about the corridor. After a minute or so, she spotted a blond head bobbing above the rest. Lori was never too hard to spot. She stood out like a pale pink rose in a field of dandelions.

Lori's long blond hair floated about her slender shoulders, seeming to radiate a glow of its own. She was wearing a pink blouse and a paisley skirt that swirled about her calves as she walked. There was something regal about her that other kids—those who didn't know her very well—sometimes tended to mistake for snobbishness. Nothing could have been further from the truth, however. Lori wasn't the least bit stuck-up. Just the opposite, in fact. She went so far out of her way to do things for others, she often ended up shortchanging herself.

Alex took off after Lori, easily dodging the jam of slower-moving bodies surrounding her. "If I didn't know better, I might think you were trying to avoid me," she said as she caught up with her friend. "How come you didn't wait?"

Lori blinked. Her enormous sky-blue eyes held a dreamy, unfocused look. They were also a little bloodshot, as if she'd been crying.

"Sorry, Alex . . . I guess I just forgot. I was thinking

about something else." Her lower lip wobbled. A tear spilled down her cheek.

Alex grabbed her elbow in concern. "What is it, Lori? What's wrong?"

Alex couldn't imagine what Lori was so upset about. She had everything a girl could possibly want: looks, popularity, friends who loved her, and a boyfriend who was both gorgeous and utterly devoted to her.

Was that it? Had Lori and Perry had a fight?

Lori ducked her head. A tear splashed onto the binder she clutched against her chest. "Oh, Alex . . . it's so awful . . . I still can't believe it. It just doesn't seem real. Perry—" She broke off with a sob.

Alex quickly steered her over to the drinking fountain, out of stampeding range. "Perry *what*?"

"He—" Again, flooded with emotion, she was unable to go on. She shook her head. More tears splattered onto her blue binder.

"Does Perry want to break up—is that it?"

Lori's head snapped up. She looked horrified at the suggestion. "No! That's not it at all. He's . . . he's moving away. His whole family. His father's company is transferring Mr. Kingston to Boston. That's what Perry wanted to talk to me about at lunchtime."

Alex felt a rush of compassion for her friend that blotted out her own worries. "Oh, Lori, that's *awful*! I don't blame you for being upset. I'd be a wreck, if that happened to me!"

"I haven't been able to stop crying since he told me," she said, sniffing.

"When is he leaving?"

"Soon. A few weeks, I guess. As soon as they can get

55

everything packed up." Lori gulped, and in a much smaller voice she added, "I just don't know how I'll ever be able to say good-bye. I *already* miss him just thinking about it!"

Alex slipped an arm about Lori's trembling shoulders. She knew how hard it was to say good-bye to someone you loved. She remembered all too well what it had been like at the hospital, when she finally had to admit that Noodle was dying and that she would never see him again. The situation with Lori and Perry wasn't the same, of course, but she could certainly sympathize.

"I know how horrible you must feel," she told Lori, "but it's not necessarily the end. You can still visit each other . . . and write. I know it'll be a lot harder, but . . . well, if you really love each other . . ." she let her reassurances trail off, knowing how weak they must have sounded to Lori.

"I know. I know. I've been telling myself all that, but . . . I still feel like I've been run over by a train. One thing's for sure—it won't be the same after he moves. We'll be three thousand miles apart. No matter how much you love someone, it's not the same when you're apart."

Alex suspected Lori was right. Hadn't she and Danny talked about the very same thing—what their lives would be like after graduation, when they left for separate colleges? They had both agreed it would probably be best to date other people once that happened, though Alex suspected the problems they were having had a lot to do with Danny being so reasonable about her dating other boys. She recalled how jealous he used to get, in the beginning of their relationship, if another boy even looked twice at her. She'd hated his jealousy then, but now she wished it could be that way again—if only to prove that he still loved her as much as ever.

Lori dabbed at her eyes with a handkerchief she'd pulled from her purse. Lori was the only girl Alex knew who brought a neatly ironed handkerchief to school each day. This one was embroidered with tiny flowers around the edges.

"I guess I'm being selfish," she said. "Perry feels just as bad about it as I do. I know I'd feel even worse if I were the one who had to move. Then I'd have to say good-bye to *everybody*, you and Kit and Elaine, instead of just him."

"I'm glad you're not moving," Alex said. She dug into her own purse for one of the man-sized Kleenex tissues she carried around with her. "Here, use this. Your handkerchief is prettier, but it's not much use for heavy-duty action. Anyway, I think you owe yourself a good cry. I know how upset *I* would be if Danny told me he was moving."

Lori blew into the Kleenex, then lifted her face to offer Alex a shaky smile. The tip of her nose was a shiny pink. "Thanks. But I'm afraid if I really get started, I won't be able to stop. I could cry enough to flood this whole school!"

"That's okay. I wouldn't mind swimming to classes for a change. It would cut down on my pool practice."

Lori gave a feeble laugh at Alex's joke. "I think what I'd really like to do right now is go home. Do you think if I told Mrs. Hartley I was sick, she'd believe me?"

Mrs. Hartley wasn't an easy one to fool. She'd been the school nurse for as long as anyone could re-

57

member and had heard every possible excuse there was, including the time Jeff Becker claimed he'd been poisoned by the cafeteria's meatloaf. But Lori *did* look pretty awful, as if she really could be sick. It was worth a try, at any rate.

"I'll walk to the office with you," Alex said. "I'll need to get a late pass for myself, anyway." Neither one had noticed the sixth period bell when it rang, but now the corridor was deserted.

Lori trudged along at Alex's side, stopping to blow into her tissue with every few steps. "I'll bet there are a lot of pretty girls in Boston," she said.

"None of them could be as pretty as you," Alex replied loyally.

Lori looked up from her Kleenex and smiled thinly. "Thanks."

"For what? I was only telling the truth. Just don't spread it around about Perry moving, or you'll have a hundred guys lining up to take his place before he's even gone."

But that only made Lori blow her nose even harder. "Oh, Alex. I don't *want* anyone else! That's just it. Even though Perry and I haven't"—she blushed— "well, you know, we're not as close in some ways as you and Danny . . . I just can't imagine going out with another boy." She bit her lip. "I'm even beginning to wonder if maybe Perry and I *should* have, well, you know, gone all the way. Especially since we'll probably never have another chance after a few weeks."

Alex was shocked. Lori was so cautious and, well, almost shy about sex. It was odd to hear her talking this way. "You're not really thinking of doing it, are you?"

"Why not? What would be so terrible about it? You and Danny do it, so do Kit and Justin."

"Kit and I aren't *you*. I just think it would be a bad idea, that's all. Not in general, I mean, but under the circumstances—with Perry moving away. Won't that just make it harder?"

"Maybe. But at least we'd have something to *really* remember each other by."

"But you already have that. Going all the way doesn't make you love someone *more*. It's the other way around. You do it *because* you love each other."

"That makes it okay, then. What could be wrong about it if Perry and I are really in love?"

Alex sighed. Ann Landers had it easy, she thought. All she had to do was hand out advice to some anonymous person. She didn't have to stick around to see how it turned out. What if she gave the wrong advice and Lori hated her for life because of it?

Gently, she said, "Maybe it is the right thing, but just the wrong time. Think about it, Lori. Don't make any snap decisions about something as important as this."

"It's not as if I have all the time in the world," Lori said. She fell silent, obviously wrapped up in thoughts of what it would be like when it came time to say good-bye.

Alex was silent, too. There were times, she knew, when no words, no matter how reassuring or well intentioned, can ease a person's misery. The best she could offer Lori was to be as supportive as possible— something Lori had always been for her when she needed it.

When they reached the administration building,

they parted ways at the door to the nurse's office. "Good luck," Alex whispered. "You'd better tell Mrs. Hartley it's terminal, or the most you'll get out of her is a couple of aspirins."

Lori gave a pained look. "I think it just might be." She sighed.

# CHAPTER SIX

"Where's the famous, or should I say *in*famous, Stephanie?" Danny asked, ambling over to where Alex, Kit, and Elaine stood waiting by the flagpole after school.

"I don't know," Alex answered irritably. They'd been waiting fifteen minutes already. "Maybe we should just leave without her."

They'd planned on dropping Kit off at Gennaro's, the pizza parlor where she worked part-time, on the way home. Kit would be late if they didn't leave pretty soon. Darn that Stephanie! Alex was sorry she'd offered to give her a ride.

Danny peered at Alex as he leaned up against the

flagpole. "I take it things still aren't going too smoothly between you two." His hair was still damp from swimming practice. He wore a pair of worn old cords, his favorite huarache sandals, and his orange Glenwood diving team sweat shirt.

"That's putting it mildly," she said.

"Isn't that her . . . over there, talking to Kirk Wallace?" Elaine pointed over to where the biker crowd stood gathered by their motorcycles a short distance away, at the entrance to the parking lot.

Alex stared over at them, frowning. Kirk was slouched up against his bike, an unlit cigarette dangling from his lower lip. He wore an old baseball jacket with the sleeves ripped out, a sort of raggedy vest that showed off his meaty arms.

One of those arms was resting about Stephanie's shoulders. Alex shuddered. She wouldn't have imagined even Stephanie could sink so low. Kirk Wallace had the worst reputation of any boy in school. His friends weren't much better, either. They were all lousy students who couldn't care less about school; most of them wore grungy-looking clothes, and some had studded leather bracelets about their wrists. The girls all looked as if they hadn't washed their hair in a year.

As Alex watched, Stephanie started to move away. Kirk tightened his hold on her arm. The expression on Stephanie's face grew angry all of a sudden. Alex couldn't hear what she was saying, but it looked as if she was telling Kirk off. Obviously, Stephanie wasn't as interested in Kirk as it had first looked.

Finally Stephanie wrenched her arm free of Kirk's

grasp and spun away, ignoring the leering taunt Kirk flung after her. For a second she looked as if she were about to cry.

Then she saw Alex and sauntered over. "You didn't have to wait," she said. "I told you I might have other plans."

"Anything to do with Kirk Wallace?" Alex asked.

Stephanie's face darkened. "Him?" she replied contemptuously. "Not hardly."

"He giving you trouble?" Danny asked, all sympathy.

"I can handle it," Stephanie said, her gaze flicking over him.

"I know him," Danny said. "He's in my shop class. A real jerk. He's always giving people a hard time. If he keeps on bothering you, let me know. I'll tell him to bug off."

"You're not afraid of him?" Elaine asked. "I hear he keeps a knife in his locker."

"He's not as tough as he'd like everyone to think," Danny said. "Besides, he wouldn't do anything to get kicked out of school. He hates it, but he practically lives for that shop class. He's always bragging about how he's going to be an auto mechanic after he graduates."

"I wanted to take shop at my last school," Stephanie said, "But they wouldn't let me. Because I'm a girl," she added in disgust.

Danny fell into step with Stephanie as they headed for his truck, which was parked way over at the far end of the parking lot. "Oh yeah? That really stinks. I know how you must have felt. I mean, I don't know *exactly*, but I can imagine. Hey, you and Alex should get along good—she's a pro at fixing that old junk heap of hers."

"That's why we're riding home in Danny's truck." Alex laughed, relieved at the easy way Danny was smoothing everything over, getting Stephanie to loosen up. "I'm so good at fixing the Green Demon that it won't even start. It's up on blocks in the garage at the moment. This time I think it might be terminal."

Everybody laughed, including—to Alex's surprise —Stephanie. It was more of a snort than a real laugh, but still, it was a start. . . .

When they got to the truck, Alex climbed into the open back with Kit and Elaine, letting Stephanie ride up in the cab with Danny. A few minutes later, when she peered in through the window, they were chattering away. Or at least, Danny was chattering, but from the expression on Stephanie's face, she appeared to be genuinely interested in what he was saying even if she wasn't saying much back.

Maybe things weren't as hopeless as she'd thought. Impetuously, she waved at Kirk Wallace as the truck swung out the parking lot exit, shooting past Kirk on his motorcycle.

Kit seized her arm with a horrified look. "What on earth did you do *that* for? Now he's going to think *you* like him." The wind had blown Kit's curls into a golden froth. Her cheeks were rosy with indignation, but her heart-shaped mouth twitched with the smile she was holding in.

Alex grinned. "Don't worry . . . I'm just thanking him."

"For what?" Elaine asked, her amber eyes round with curiosity.

"For showing me there's hope for Stephanie yet. If she'd gone home with Kirk, I'd have given her up as a totally lost cause!"

"Just don't get too carried away, thanking him." Kit laughed, scooping her curls out of her eyes. "All you need is Kirk Wallace tearing up your front lawn with his motorcycle."

A few minutes later, the truck pulled up in front of Gennaro's. They all clambered out.

"Anybody feel like pizza?" Danny asked heartily. "My treat."

"You must have read my mind," Stephanie said.

"Mine, too," Elaine piped. "My homework will have to wait. I feel a pepperoni attack coming on."

Alex edged in between Danny and Stephanie, who were standing side by side. She slipped her arm through his. "Sounds good to me. But you don't have to worry about paying for it all. I've got money." From the very beginning of their relationship, Alex had always insisted their dates be Dutch treat. It was only fair. After all, why should someone be obligated to pay for everything just because he'd been born a boy?

Danny frowned. "I *want* to pay. Listen, I know you're a hotshot women's libber and all, but sometimes a person wants to do something not because he's a guy, but just *because*." His tone was light, but Alex could sense the annoyance underneath.

Alex felt embarrassed at being put down in front of her friends. She hadn't meant any harm. Why was Danny suddenly pulling this macho act? Was it because of Stephanie? Nevertheless, she decided it would be best just to laugh it off.

"Okay, Tarzan," she shot back, "Have it your way. I was just trying to save you from utter bankruptcy. You have no idea how much pizza three hungry girls can eat, especially when they're on diets."

"Speaking of diets, what happened to Lori?" Elaine asked as they were settling into their favorite booth in the corner, beside the two video games. Kit had gone scurrying off toward the kitchen, propelled by the dirty look she'd gotten from her boss when she walked in.

Alex explained to the others what had happened to Lori. "She was so upset, she had to go home. I feel so sorry for her!"

Elaine looked shocked. "What a horrible thing to happen! Just when things were going so great between them, too. Life is so unfair!"

Stephanie, who had been pretty quiet up until now, surprised them all when she spoke out bitterly, "You guys are something else, you know that? You act like the worst thing in the world is having some dumb boyfriend move away. Big deal. I'll tell you what's really rotten—this girl I know, she was only six years old when she went into her first foster home. She was beaten up by her foster father, and they let him off because he said it was *her* fault. She was, let me see, how did he put it—oh yeah, *incorrigible.* Six years old. Incorrigible. I'll bet she didn't even know what it meant."

They all sat there, shocked into silence by Stephanie's outpouring. Even Alex couldn't think of a thing to say. Danny was the first one to speak.

"That *is* rotten," he said softly. Stephanie sat opposite him and Alex, next to Elaine. He touched the back of her hand, which was so tightly clenched her knuckles were white. "But you can't go through life concentrating on all the bad stuff. There's so much bad stuff, it'd just drive you crazy. I mean, we could all be blown off the face of this earth the next minute by nuclear missiles, if you want to get right down to it. Maybe it's just a lot easier to worry about the small stuff."

To Alex's surprise, Stephanie had no sharp comeback to Danny's words. She merely stared at him thoughtfully, her coppery-brown eyes huge in her delicate-boned face. She relaxed her clenched hand. Softly, so softly it was almost inaudible, she said, "Yeah . . . maybe you're right."

There was an uncomfortable moment in which none of them knew what to say, then suddenly the tension broke and they were all talking at once.

"Smell that pizza!" Danny cried. "I can taste it already. I hope Kit remembered to put extra cheese on it."

Alex took a deep breath, savoring the smoky scent. "Speaking of food, what was that fishy stuff they served us for lunch today? It tasted like old sneakers that'd been put through a meat grinder."

"Is that why they call it filet of sole?" Stephanie joked.

Everybody laughed.

Alex relaxed. Danny was obviously having a good effect on Stephanie. He'd gotten her to open up and respond in a way Alex wouldn't have thought possible.

At the same time, she couldn't help feeling a small, jealous chill of apprehension at the intense way

Stephanie was looking at him. Was it just her imagination, or was Stephanie interested in Danny as something more than just a friend?

She quickly pushed the thought aside. It was ridiculous for her to feel this way, she told herself. Didn't she have enough real worries without getting jealous over what was probably nothing at all?

"Have you ever been on a camp-out?" Alex asked Stephanie later on that night, as they were getting ready for bed.

Alex sat on the toilet lid in the bathroom they shared, her knees pulled up against her chest under the loose jersey nightgown she wore. Stephanie wore only a man's T-shirt, torn at the shoulder. She didn't own a nightgown and had refused Alex's attempts to lend her one.

Stephanie stopped in the midst of brushing her teeth. "Sure . . . if you want to call running away from home camping out. I've spent a few nights by the side of the road, only it wasn't the Girl Scouts. I wasn't exactly toasting marshmallows over a campfire."

Alex sighed in exasperation. "I don't mean like in the Girl Scouts. I belong to the Junior Sierra Club. It's a lot more rugged. We hike up into the mountains with backpacks. Sometimes it's just for the day, but once in a while we go on overnight trips."

"Sounds like a lot of hard work for nothing," Stephanie commented with a shrug.

She rinsed out her toothbrush and jammed it into the holder. Alex noticed she hadn't bothered to wipe away the foam that flecked the basin, or to put the cap back on the toothpaste. Living with Stephanie, she'd found, meant constantly having to pick up after her.

Alex sighed again. She was determined to get Stephanie interested in *something* . . . even if it killed her. Besides, Chuck Hadley was going on this camp-out, too. Encouraged by Stephanie's response to Danny, Alex was hoping she could get her foster sister to warm to Chuck as well.

"It's not like that," she said. "It's a lot of fun. And the people are great, too."

"Yeah? Well, I'm not really into joining clubs."

"That's the nice thing about the Sierra Club. You don't have to socialize if you don't feel like it," Alex pushed on dauntlessly. "Some people go on hikes to sort of be alone with nature, if you know what I mean."

"I'm not a nature freak, either."

Alex gritted her teeth. "It's good exercise."

Stephanie grabbed a brush and began attacking her long dark hair until it crackled about her head in a fury of static. "Look . . . I've already told you. You don't have to include me in everything you do. Don't get offended or anything—it's just the way I am. I guess I'm a loner."

This was going to be a lot tougher than Alex had expected. "That's too bad. Danny and I were really hoping you would want to go. We're going on an overnight trip next weekend.

Stephanie stopped brushing her hair. "Danny's going, too?"

Alex wasn't sure what to think of *that*, but she decided to play it cool. "Sure. He's one of the charter members. Talk about a nature freak! Danny even knows a lot of stuff like what to eat if you get stuck out in the wilds with no trail mix. The last time we went, he fried up a batch of wild mushrooms. Only no one would eat them. Everybody was afraid of getting poisoned. Danny got so mad, he ate the whole batch himself."

A smile tugged at the corners of Stephanie's mouth. "Yeah. I could see him doing that." She spoke affectionately of Danny, as if he were an old friend, instead of someone she'd just met today.

"Lots of other boys are going, too," Alex said, trying to sound as casual as possible. "I mean, it's really a great way to meet guys. If you're interested, that is."

"I'll think about it," Stephanie said.

Alex was surprised. What had changed her mind so suddenly? Was it knowing that Danny would be coming along? Or the prospect of meeting other boys? Maybe Stephanie was more interested in romance than she let on. Alex wasn't sure what to think. Instead of feeling elated at her partial success in convincing Stephanie to join the hike, she felt a gnawing edge of uncertainty about the whole thing. Maybe she should just let Stephanie alone.

An image of Danny rose in her mind: sunny, blue-eyed Danny. Every girl's dream. A walking commercial for romance. The kind of boy they featured in blue-jeans ads with no shirt on. Or in sexy toothpaste ads. What girl *wouldn't* be interested in him?

A terrible impulse swept over Alex. She wanted to blurt out: *Keep away from Danny, he's mine!* She didn't know what had come over her. She'd never felt real jealousy having to do with Danny before; he'd certainly given her no reason to in the past.

It was silly, she told herself. Completely dumb. She was going off the deep end over nothing. Instead of thinking about Danny, she focused on Chuck Hadley. She'd won the first battle—getting Stephanie at least halfway interested in going on the Sierra Club hike. Now all she had to do was engineer a way to get her interested in Chuck. Because the more interested she got in someone else, the less interested she would be in Danny.

# CHAPTER SEVEN

"I just don't think Chuck's her type," Danny said. He scooped up another handful of sand, adding it to the pile in front of him.

"How do you *know* he's not her type?" Alex persisted.

They sat on the beach, hunched against the wind that was blowing in from the ocean. It had been Alex's idea to drive out to their favorite cove after school on Wednesday. It seemed as though they hardly saw each other anymore. And now that Danny was dropping off the diving team, they would see each other even less.

Their time together was so precious . . . and yet here they were, arguing again. How had it started? All she'd done was suggest he talk to Chuck about going out with Stephanie. Danny knew Chuck better than she did. It made perfect sense, arranging a blind date between Chuck and Stephanie. Why didn't Danny see it?

"Chuck's a nice enough guy. I'm not putting him down," Danny said. "I'm just not so sure he'd be all that sensitive to Stephanie. What she doesn't need right now is another problem in her life."

How did Danny know so much about Stephanie's problems? Alex wondered. And why should he care so much, anyway? He hardly knew her. What did it matter to him who she went out with?

She ran her tongue over her lips. There was some sand sticking to the corner of her mouth. She caught herself remembering the time she and Danny had almost made love on this beach, how he'd carefully brushed all the sand from her face before kissing her.

He hadn't kissed her once since they'd gotten here. There was no one else on the beach. They could've taken off their clothes and run around naked if they'd wanted to.

"Okay." She sighed. "So maybe Chuck's not the most sensitive guy in the world, but he's a lot of fun, and he likes to have a good time. I'm not saying they have to go steady or anything. It's just one date."

Danny was silent. He continued scooping up sand. A hole had formed in front of him big enough to bury someone's foot in. Finally, he said, "I'll ask him. But I'm not so sure he'll go for it. Stephanie may not be his type, either."

"If you put it to him that way, he'll probably run in the other direction."

Danny's head snapped. "Look, I said I'd ask. I'm not making any promises about how it'll turn out, that's all."

"Fine." Alex withdrew, stung. She watched him dig awhile longer, then said. "You're still mad about what I said to you about dropping off the team, aren't you?"

"I'm not mad," he said. "I just wish . . . ." He broke off.

"What?"

"Look, Alex, I don't want another argument. Let's just forget it, okay?"

"I don't want to forget it! If you're still mad, I want to know."

Danny faced her. His eyes had taken on the gray-blue color of the fog that was creeping in from the ocean. His expression was very still and unsmiling.

"I'm not mad," he repeated. "It's . . . well, if you want to know . . . it's the way you're always trying to run everybody's life, mainly mine—it really gets to me sometimes."

"I'm not trying to run your life!" she cried, hurt. "I was just trying to keep you from making a mistake. Danny, you've been with the team so long . . . to give it up now would be such a waste."

"Face it, Alex. I'm not as good as you are. I never have been. I never will be."

"You could be, if you tried!"

"Maybe. The point is, I don't have . . . well, whatever it is that drives you so hard. The truth is, I've been wanting to drop off the team for a while. The only reason I stayed was because of you . . . because I knew how much it meant to you."

*Then why now?* she wanted to ask, but didn't dare.

What if he said he was dropping out now because he no longer cared how she felt?

"What did Coach Reeves say when you told him?" she asked, curling her toes about a piece of dried seaweed.

She stared out at the ocean, which looked stormier than usual today. The waves were huge, shooting long fingers of foam into the air as they exploded against the rocks ringing the shore.

"Not much," he said. "I don't think he was too surprised, after all the practice sessions I've skipped. Anyway, I'm no great loss to the team. We both know that."

Alex turned back to Danny. "We won't see each other as much."

"Sure we will! It's not as if we go to different schools or anything."

Danny didn't understand how she felt at all. Was she the only one who saw what was happening to them? She felt as if they were both standing on the railroad tracks, but she was the only one who could see the train coming at them.

It wasn't just the team. It was everything. She longed for things to be the way they used to be between them.

Maybe it wasn't too late. Maybe she could still fix it.

Alex scooted over so that she was in front of Danny, sitting cross-legged with the hole between them. She reached into it and gouged out a chunk of cold, damp sand with her fingers.

"What are you doing?" he asked.

"If you're going to dig your way to China, I might as well help," she said.

"I should have known."

"Unless you were planning on going there without me." She tilted her head, gazing at him in mock defiance.

"Not a chance."

Alex pushed back the hair that had blown into her eyes. "You know, when I was younger, I believed it really was possible to dig your way to China."

He laughed. "If it were, you'd be the first to do it."

"Uh, I hope you don't mind, but Danny said he might bring a friend along," Alex told Stephanie Friday night as they were getting ready to go out.

There. It was out. She'd been practicing saying it with just the right amount of offhandedness ever since Danny had informed her that Chuck was willing to go out with Stephanie. Alex had arranged their double date for tonight.

The only problem was, she hadn't told Stephanie. Knowing her, she would probably back out if she knew it was going to be a blind date. Once she got to know Chuck, it would be different. But for now it was best if she thought he was just joining their threesome as an afterthought.

Stephanie paused in the middle of tugging her boots on over her jeans. She looked up at Alex, who stood in the doorway. "Who?" she demanded.

"His name's Chuck Hadley. He . . ." She was on the verge of blurting out that he was tall, fairly handsome, and on the track team, but she bit her tongue. Stephanie would get suspicious if she said too much. ". . . goes to Glenwood. Maybe you know him."

Stephanie shook her head. "I thought it was going

to be just the three of us. If you'd told me—"

Alex didn't give her a chance to finish. "I know we planned it that way, but this just sort of came up at the last minute. Actually, Chuck was the one who asked Danny if he wanted to get together, so Danny just naturally invited him along. You don't mind, do you?"

Stephanie finished pulling on her boots. "Nah. I guess not. When you put it that way." She seemed in a better mood than usual tonight. A good sign.

She looked nicer, too, Alex noted. She wore her usual pair of jeans but had substituted a silky blue top in place of her usual T-shirt and denim jacket. She'd even curled her hair. Fluffed up around her face, it made her features look softer, her bones not quite so sharp.

"Great!" Alex said, fighting to keep her relief from showing. Quickly, she added, "I mean, it's no big thing. It's not like a date or anything. . . ."

"Listen, Alex," Stephanie interrupted, "I was wondering if . . . uh . . . well, if you don't mind, could I use some of your mascara?" She looked down at the rug instead of at Alex.

Alex grinned. This was the first time Stephanie had ever asked to borrow anything of hers. She hoped it was a sign that they were making progress.

Then another, nastier, thought crept in: Why the sudden interest in glamorizing herself? Who was she trying to impress? Danny?

She quickly banished the thought, ashamed of herself for being so suspicious.

"Sure," she said. "It's in the bathroom. Help yourself."

"Thanks," Stephanie mumbled, hastily ducking past her.

Alex could hear Stephanie in the bathroom, rattling around in the medicine cabinet. "Top shelf!" she called out on her way back to her own bedroom.

A few minutes later, Stephanie showed up in Alex's room, mascara wand in hand. "Uh . . . the thing is . . . I've never used this stuff before." Her voice was gruff with the effort of having to ask for help.

Alex sprang forward. "Here, let me show you. It's not hard."

Stephanie tilted her head back with an embarrassed laugh. "I should know how just from watching Paula goop this stuff on all the time. She wore so much makeup, she looked like some kind of vampire."

Alex giggled as she attempted to guide the wand over Stephanie's lashes, which were so naturally dark and thick, they hardly needed any mascara.

"Paula sounds like a real creep, from everything you've told me. Were all your foster families that bad?"

"Some were okay. The lady before Paula's family— she was nice."

"Why didn't you stay with her?"

"She got sick, she had to go into the hospital."

"Oh, that's too bad. Is she okay now? I mean, she's not still sick is she?"

"I don't know. After the welfare people sent me to live with the Schroeders, I sort of lost touch."

"You should write her a letter," Alex suggested. "Just to find out how she is, and let her know you're okay."

"Maybe I will," Stephanie said.

They were interrupted by the chiming of the door-bell. Then Alex's mother called, "Alex! Stephanie! Danny and his friend are here."

"Coming!" Alex called back.

She hastily checked her own appearance in the mirror. She'd put on a dress for a change—a striped yellow halter dress that showed off the dusky hue of her skin. Would Danny like it? They were only going to a movie, but tonight she wanted to look her best for him.

Danny was leaning up against the piano when she came into the living room. Chuck, who was sitting on the couch, jumped to his feet. He was so tall, he nearly grazed the ceiling. He grinned, his gaze fastening on Stephanie. There was a slight gap between his front teeth, which Alex had never noticed before.

Alex introduced them. "Chuck . . . this is Stephanie."

Stephanie nodded in his direction, but she hung back as if afraid of being paired up with him.

Chuck didn't seem to notice. "It's really great to meet you," he said. "You know, I've seen you around school . . . and I'd been hoping we'd run into each other, so when Danny-boy here called me and asked if I wanted to—"

"Danny called *you?*" Stephanie broke in with a horrified expression. She looked over at Danny as if she couldn't believe he would do this to her.

"It was my idea," Alex volunteered. She was hoping she could appeal to the Stephanie who had seemed willing to accept her friendship only moments before. "I wanted to surprise you."

Stephanie glared at her. "I don't like surprises." Her

voice was cold and hard. "You set me up. You lied to me."

"I was only trying to . . ."

But Stephanie wouldn't let her explain. She spun about, darting back down the hallway. Alex heard her bedroom door slam shut.

She was so embarrassed, she didn't know what to say. She was grateful her parents weren't in the room to witness the scene. Her father was in the den, and her mother must have gone back into the kitchen.

Chuck cleared his throat. "Hey, I'm really sorry if I said the wrong thing. I didn't know the score." His face was red.

"It wasn't your fault, Chuck." She turned to Danny, unable to hide the accusation in her voice. "Danny should have told you."

Danny shifted uncomfortably, shoving his hands into the pockets of his khaki trousers. "I guess I don't like setups, either," he said defensively. "Look, Alex, I'm sorry about the way it turned out, but . . . I never thought it was such a good idea to begin with."

"You're saying the whole thing is my fault!"

"I didn't say that."

"I think I should wait out in the car," muttered Chuck, heading for the front door.

Danny went over to Alex. "I know you meant well. Maybe if I talked to Stephanie, it would help."

Something inside Alex snapped. "I don't care about Stephanie! I'm sick of tiptoeing around her feelings! Don't I have feelings, too?"

He put his arms around her. "I care about your feelings, Alex. But you have to admit, this whole thing might've turned out differently if you'd been more

81

honest with her. I just thought if I talked to her, sort of explained how you meant well . . ."

Alex slumped against him, her anger spent. He was right. She should have been more honest with Stephanie. She should have realized how Stephanie would feel about being set up, after a lifetime of setups with strange families.

But that still didn't excuse the way Stephanie had blown up in front of Chuck . . . or the traitorous way Danny was defending her.

She thought about how chummy Danny and Stephanie had gotten lately. This past week, whenever Danny had been over at her house, Stephanie always managed to horn in. One night when Alex had to study for a test, Danny and Stephanie had gone into the den to watch TV together.

Stephanie was far from outgoing, but she always perked up whenever Danny was around. She listened to what he had to say and laughed at his jokes, even when they weren't funny.

All those jealous thoughts came flooding over her in a green tidal wave as Alex followed Danny down the hall and watched him disappear into Stephanie's bedroom.

She could hear the low murmur of voices inside. She pictured Danny with his arm about Stephanie, consoling her. Stephanie with her head resting against his shoulder. Hating herself for doing so, she strained to hear what they were saying. But the words were indistinguishable. Were they talking about her, agreeing with each other about how thoughtless she was?

82

Finally, she couldn't stand it any longer. She went into her own room and flopped down on the bed. There was a pain in her stomach that wouldn't go away. But she was too upset even to cry.

Alex wasn't sure who she resented more at this moment— Stephanie or Danny.

# CHAPTER EIGHT

Alex lay flat on her back, buried in the grimy depths of the Green Demon. A slender, scarlet-nailed hand fluttered into her line of vision, clutching a blue envelope.

"Look what my mom's boyfriend gave me!" Kit's excited voice filtered down.

All Alex could see of her was a pair of high-heeled red sandals and the ankle-hugging cuffs of her jeans.

Alex scooted out from underneath her car, wrench in hand, pausing to push a strand of hair out of her eyes with the back of her wrist, the only part of her that wasn't covered in grease.

Kit squatted on her haunches beside the Dodge,

grinning. She wore an oversized blue chambray work-shirt untucked over her jeans, which she'd cunningly accented with a wide red leather sash. Her irrepressible blond curls were tied up on top of her head in a loose topknot from which a froth of tendrils escaped about her neck and ears.

Alex eyed the tickets in Kit's hand. "What are they for?"

"The race on Saturday over at the Laguna track. Steve says it's the biggest auto race of the year around here," Kit explained, quoting her mother's boyfriend as an authority. "Sort of like the Indy 500 of northern California. He knows all about stuff like that. He's one of the sponsors."

"I've heard of it," Alex said. She was interested in any sport of which speed was the main ingredient. "Isn't that the one where a guy got hurt last year?"

"Steve says the description in the papers made it sound worse than it really was. The driver had some broken bones, but he's back competing in this year's race. Wes Thorsen's his name, I think. I hear he's the favorite to win."

"Sounds like fun," Alex said, though she sighed inwardly. She hadn't been able to get too excited about much of anything these past few days; she was still depressed over what had happened Friday night. Neither she nor Stephanie had ended up going out anywhere at all. "How many tickets did you get?"

"Four. Enough for all of us. I wanted Justin to come, too, but he's going to be busy this Saturday." Kit screwed her heart-shaped face up in a comical pout. "They're training him for that laboratory job he's taking this summer. Some kind of special seminar. Anyway, just because he's off somewhere grinding away doesn't mean *I* can't have fun."

Alex sat up, tossing down her wrench. Kit was right. The fate of the world didn't rest on their boyfriends. No matter how she felt about Danny, she shouldn't let it interfere with having a good time.

"Great. I'm not doing anything on Saturday as far as I know. I'd love to go. I've seen enough auto races on *Wide World of Sports*. It's about time I caught the live act."

Kit cast a sidelong glance at Alex's battered green Dodge. Her blue eyes sparkled with fun. "Are you sure you wouldn't like to compete yourself? Maybe we should enter the Green Demon in the race."

"Great. I've always wanted to know what it would be like to come in last."

Kit laughed. "That's one experience *you'll* never have!" She was always joking that Alex, a fierce competitor when it came to any kind of athletic event, couldn't come in last even if she broke every bone in her body.

Alex got up and began shoving her tools into the big dented toolbox at her side. "At the rate I'm going with this dumb car, I'd be lucky even to get it off the starting line. Last week it was the differential. Now there's something wrong with the alternator."

Kit rolled her eyes as she straightened, leaning up against the car on one hip. "Sounds like one of the equations we have to solve in calculus, only a lot messier." She shot a meaningful glance at Alex's grimy coveralls.

Alex had found her big blue coveralls ages ago at the Salvation Army. They were at least two sizes too big and had the name "Mac" sewn onto the pocket. Her friends told Alex all she needed when she was wearing them was a mustache to look like Charlie Chaplin. But Alex loved them. They were roomy and comfortable, and she could get as dirty in them as she wanted. She didn't care how fashionable she looked. Comfort occupied first place where her wardrobe was concerned.

"What about Lori and Elaine?" Alex asked. "Are they going?"

"I called them before I came over. Lori can't—she's got a date with Perry. They're making every last minute count. Elaine's not wild about car races, but she said she'd go if you would."

"Is Lori still as depressed as ever?" Alex wanted to know.

Today was Tuesday. Lori had been drifting about since last week, looking like the heroine from some tragic novel. She sighed a lot and scarcely ate anything. Whenever she was with Perry, the two clung to each other like a pair of shipwreck survivors.

"She was pretty down when I talked to her," Kit said thoughtfully. She found a seat amid the clutter of Alex's garage on an old overturned canoe. "It's hard finding things to say that will cheer her up. I just keep thinking of how I'd feel if it was Justin. But I guess that's something we'll all have to face someday soon, when we go away to college."

"Well, the way I look at it, going away to college is so monumental it'll probably take our minds off saying good-bye when the time comes. Temporarily, at least. It's harder, I think, being the one left behind."

Alex had thought about graduating a lot. She'd applied to several different colleges, none of them close to home. Since Danny was more interested in computers than athletic training these days, he hadn't applied to any of the same colleges she had. She felt a pang at the thought of what it would be like when it came time for them to say good-bye.

How could she feel this way, when she was still mad at Danny? It was crazy, how you could love someone and yet still feel they were wrong for you in a hundred different ways.

Nothing had been the same since Friday night, though they were acting as if everything were normal. What was the use of fighting? It wouldn't solve anything . . . it would only drive them further apart.

Love made no sense at all. Even with all the books that had been written about it, and the songs composed about the subject, no one had figured it out yet.

And then there was Stephanie.

Alex had been so furious with her foster sister over the incident on Friday night, and vice versa, that they'd barely spoken two words to each other all weekend. Not that things had ever been smooth between them. But what had been a battle before was now all-out war.

"How's Stephanie?" Kit asked, as if she'd read Alex's mind.

Alex groaned. "Don't ask."

"That bad?"

"Worse."

"Are you still mad at her for the way she walked out on the blind date you fixed up for her?"

"That's only part of it. The other ninety percent is her general obnoxiousness. Honestly, Kit, I just don't know how much longer I can put up with it! It's not just me . . . it's Mom and Dad, too. She acts as if she can't stand any of us."

"What about Danny? She likes him, doesn't she?"

Alex hadn't confided her jealousy to her friends yet. She couldn't bring herself to talk about it, period. Deep down, she was afraid that if she put her suspicions into words, that would somehow make it real instead of hopefully just imaginary.

She fished a rag from one of her voluminous pockets and began furiously wiping her hands. There was a rim of grime embedded below her thumbnail. She dug at it with the sharp point of a nail she'd found lying nearby.

"Who doesn't like Danny?" She laughed. "A person would have to be made of stone not to like him."

"Especially a person of the female gender," Kit joked innocently.

Alex concentrated even harder on her thumbnail. "It's not like that. They're just—ow!" The nail slipped, gouging into the tender flesh of her thumb. Alex winced as a ruby droplet of blood oozed to the surface.

Kit jumped up. "You're bleeding!"

"It's nothing."

Kit followed Alex through the garage door into the kitchen. At the sink, Alex ran warm water over her gouged hand, washing it thoroughly so it wouldn't get infected.

"I'll get the Mercurochrome," Kit said, dashing toward the bathroom, where Alex's mother kept a first aid kit.

"It's just a pinprick!" Alex yelled after her in protest.

"I don't want you dying of tetanus or anything," Kit called back, eventually returning with a small red bottle. She dabbed Mercurochrome onto Alex's cut. "I'd have it on my conscience for the rest of my life."

Alex flinched. "It stings."

"It's supposed to sting. That means it's working. At least that's what my mother always told me."

"Mothers always say that. I think it's just a way of easing the process when they're torturing us."

"I couldn't find the Band-Aids. Do you have any?" Kit asked when she'd finished painting Alex's thumb scarlet. They stood in the Enomotos' big sunny kitchen, with its yellow checkered curtains and the row of African violets lined up on the windowsill over the sink.

"I don't need a Band-Aid." Alex laughed. "Will you quit acting like I've been mortally wounded!"

Kit shrugged. "Okay. But if us latch-key kids don't take care of each other, who will?" Before Alex could reply, she glanced at her watch and cried, "Uh-oh, I've gotta run. I promised Justin I'd meet him at the library—he's helping me out with my term paper for government." She made a face. "Talk about romantic! You know how long you've been going together when your boyfriend would rather study naval battles of World War II than make out in his car."

"I know the feeling." Alex laughed. Last time she and Danny had gotten together for a study date, they'd actually *studied.*

After Kit had gone, Alex went into her room to finish her homework. But she couldn't concentrate. Stephanie had the radio turned up full blast. The wall separating their rooms seemed to throb with the noise.

When she couldn't stand it any longer, she got up

and marched into Stephanie's room.

"Will you turn it *down*?" she yelled.

Stephanie lay stretched out on her back on the bed, wearing shorts and a Grateful Dead T-shirt she'd picked up at the flea market on Saturday. She made no move to get up or even acknowledge Alex's presence.

Alex stalked over and flipped off the radio.

Stephanie sat up, scowling. "Hey, what'd you do that for?"

"I couldn't concentrate on my homework with all the noise."

"You didn't have to turn it all the way off!" Stephanie got up and snapped it back on—turning it up even louder than before.

Fury boiled up inside Alex. This time she didn't just flip the switch, she unplugged the radio with a hard yank on the cord. "You're not the only one living here!" she said.

They faced each other like two gunfighters squaring off for a duel. Alex stood with her hands braced against her hips. Stephanie's arms were folded across her chest, her eyes narrowed in a hard squint.

"Yeah, well, I never asked to live here at all!" she flung back at Alex.

"I know. You've told me a zillion times. Well, you're just going to have to put up with us . . . for Mom and Dad's sake, if not mine."

"They don't want me here any more than you do, I'll bet."

"Why don't you try acting like you want to stick around, instead of putting all the blame on us?"

"Maybe I don't plan on sticking around," Stephanie threatened.

Alex was on the verge of shouting, *so what's stopping you from leaving?* But she bit her tongue. That was going too far. Besides, she'd promised Mom and Dad she would make a real attempt to curb her temper as far as Stephanie was concerned.

She turned away with a tight shrug, kicking at the cord that snaked across the carpet at her feet. Stephanie bent down and, in one swift movement, plugged it back in again. Noise exploded from the radio.

Alex stomped out of the room.

# CHAPTER NINE

"I know exactly how you feel," Elaine commiserated, twisting around to face Alex from the front seat of Kit's VW bug. "My sisters are like that sometimes. There are times when I honestly feel like strangling them."

Elaine was dressed for a day at the racetrack in off-white slacks and a sleeveless cotton sweater in a bold zigzag pattern. Her sleek brown hair was scooped back in a ponytail that flipped up into the air every time Kit, who was a nervous driver, stamped on the brakes.

"It's not the same for Alex," Kit pointed out, guiding her VW into the crowded parking lot at the Laguna racetrack. "Stephanie's not her real sister, so strangling is out. That's only allowed if you're related by blood."

"Thanks." Elaine grinned. "I'll remember that next time Andy sneaks a peek at my diary. Not"—she sighed—"that there's anything in it worth getting excited about. My diary would probably put most people to sleep."

"In some ways, it'd be easier if Stephanie *was* my real sister," Alex reflected. "Then we could get mad at each other all we wanted because there'd be nothing we could do to change the fact that we'd always be sisters."

"I'm glad I don't have any sisters." Kit said. "Looking after my mother is enough as it is."

She nosed toward a parking space, then discovered she was going in at the wrong angle and had to back out and start again. As she rammed the stick into reverse, the car lurched, then died. Kit laughed, unperturbed. She'd be the first one to admit she wasn't the world's best driver. In fact, after Alex started calling her Dodge the "Green Demon" she often joked that she should call her orange VW the "Pokey Pumpkin."

Alex braced herself as the VW jerked forward, died once again, then finally sputtered into the parking space. Directly ahead loomed the grandstands, surrounded by cyclone fencing, through which she could see a section of the oval track. A sleek numbered car zipped past, hugging the inside lane.

"They're doing their test runs," Alex said. "Come on, let's hurry up and find our seats. I don't want to miss any of it!"

She loved watching races on TV, so she knew a lot

about it even though she'd never actually been to a live race. Her pulse quickened as she approached the front gate, and the noise of the crowd, combined with the snarling of engines and the hot smell of grease, swept over her. Watching *Sportsworld* couldn't even begin to capture all of this.

Today especially she longed to lose herself in something different and exciting. She didn't want to think about her problems with Danny or Stephanie . . . if only for a few hours.

Up in the grandstands, they found their seats, squeezing in beside two men and a fat woman eating a hot dog. Just in time. The race was about to begin.

Alex squinted against the harsh sunlight, gazing down at the track. The cars were lined up in their pole positions—all of them sleek and swift-looking. The sound made by their engines, set at a racing idle, sent a thrill chasing up her spine. The sun beat down on her head, and a bead of sweat trickled down between her shoulder blades.

Suddenly, the noise of the crowd fell to a sudden hush, as if a volume-control knob had been turned down. The air was filled with the smell of hot rubber, popcorn, perspiring bodies.

Alex noticed Kit scanning the crowd for a sign of her mother and Steve, who would be down in one of the pits, but she saw no sign of either. There was too much activity—men in grease-stained overalls, photographers snapping pictures, TV crews with their mini-cams.

Alex had her eye on one car in particular—number nineteen. It was silver and shaped like a bullet. The sun reflecting off the gleaming hood gave it a sleek and dangerous look the others didn't have. Alex's gaze was held by it, as if hypnotized. It seemed more impatient than the others, edging toward the starting line, then falling back, forward and back. Whoever the driver was behind the wheel, it was obvious he couldn't wait to get started.

*I know the feeling!* Alex thought, her heart picking up the throbbing tempo of the engines. That was exactly how she felt at meets before she dove. Watching others take their turns before her, she would itch to feel the rasp of the fiberglass board against her bare soles, to feel the coiled spring of her body release as she sailed out over the turquoise water, arching and twisting.

She glanced back over at Kit, who seemed to have shrunk. Kit was scrunched down in her seat, trying to avoid the obvious stares of several men surrounding them. Alex and Elaine exchanged amused looks. Elaine looked more glowingly confident than ever. Now that she was secure about her own appearance, she didn't have to feel jealous when voluptuous Kit attracted the lion's share of attention.

Alex turned her attention back to the track just in time to see the flash of the green flag, signaling the start of the race. Her whole body gave a little jump as the numbered cars hurtled forward, a blur of colors amid swirling smoke and dust.

Her gaze remained riveted to the gleaming silver car with number nineteen painted on its side. It seemed more aggressive than the others, for one thing. Shooting ahead of the other cars by a narrow lead, it zoomed into the first curve, hugging the inside track. Alex held her breath as another car overtook it, their sides brushing so close she could almost imagine the shriek of metal and flying sparks.

"I can't watch," murmured Elaine. Her eyes were screwed shut. "Somebody's going to get killed. I just know it."

Alex fumbled for Elaine's hand, giving it a reassuring squeeze. She felt queasy with fear, too, but that only doubled her fascination. Speed. Danger. Excitement. Those things thrilled and challenged her in a way she could never explain to someone who hadn't ever felt the same way she did. It was one of the reasons Danny had never fully understood her. Taking chances was a way of life for her, but to him, they were often an unnecessary risk.

The feeling she had now was so intense, her body swayed each time the cars swung into a bend. Her hands clenched about an invisible wheel as they tore down the straightaway at top speed. She was right there inside number nineteen, sweating it out alongside the driver.

Several cars dropped out due to mechanical difficulties. Alex held her breath as one car skewed wildly going into a turn, fishtailing off the track in a plume of smoking rubber. Number nineteen held on to its narrow lead against number four—a pug-nosed racer with a broad yellow stripe slashing its side. As the two edged against each other in the final lap, the crowd grew tense. A kind of electricity hung in the air.

Number four pulled ahead slightly. The last curve loomed ahead. Both cars seemed to dig their tires in as they angled into it, unwilling to slack off their speed. There was the high squeal of tires. Number nineteen was pulling close again; they were side by side. The curve threw them together until they were almost touching. The sun no longer gleamed off their dusty bodies. They were just two exhausted survivors gritting their teeth at the end, determined not to give in.

Nineteen spurted ahead half a car's length. The checkered flag swooped down. The race was over.

The crowd went wild.

Alex felt herself being propelled forward as people poured down off the stands. She and her friends were close to the front, caught up in the first wave. The pits were cordoned off, but somehow Kit managed to get one of the ogling attendants to let them sneak through so she could look for her mother.

Suddenly, Alex found herself on the fringes of the winner's circle, among the crowd of people pressing forward to congratulate the driver of number nineteen. She stared at him as he climbed out of the dust-streaked car, tearing off his helmet in one swift movement.

Her first impression was of a grin that more than matched the brilliance of the trophy that someone shoved into his gloved hand. His black hair clung to his forehead in damp tendrils. His eyes were a light greenish color fringed with dark lashes. He wasn't tall, but he had a sturdy muscularity that conveyed power and determination even standing still. He wasn't very old, either; he didn't look much older than she. Alex found herself just as mesmerized by the driver as she had been by his car during the race.

Alex heard the loud pop of a champagne cork close to her ear. The man next to her jumped, jostling her elbow. Alex stepped forward to get out of his way, and found herself standing right next to the driver. Then suddenly they were both caught in a soapy cascade of champagne. Alex was so stunned she couldn't even move. The cold liquid dribbled down her head onto her T-shirt.

The boy turned the radiance of his grin on Alex. White flecks of champagne bubbles stood out on his dark hair. His light-green eyes danced with mischief. There was something utterly irresistible about his devil-may-care expression that made Alex want to laugh out loud.

Unexpectedly, he grabbed her hand. "Come on. We'd better get out of here before we're both drenched."

Alex wanted to protest that they didn't even know each other. But it was too late. His sturdy fingers had already tightened over hers, and he was running, ducking toward the row of garages beyond the pit with Alex in tow. Even for her, it was a struggle to keep up.

"My name's Wes, what's yours!" he shouted above the clamor of the crowd.

"Alex!" she shouted back.

Alex had been only dimly aware of the startled expressions on the faces of her friends as she was dragged off. She heard a whirring sound and half-turned to see a mini-cam pointed straight at her. They ducked under a shady overhang. Cool. Dark. The smell of fuel. They had reached the safety of the garage. Wes pulled the corrugated metal door shut.

"Sorry about kidnapping you like that," he apologized, his dimpled grin denying that he was sorry. "I don't know what came over me. I guess I'm not much for the crowd scene, and when I saw you dripping with champagne, you gave me a good excuse to duck out. Knight in armor to the rescue!" Casually, he tossed aside the trophy he'd just won onto a box piled high with grease-stained rags.

Alex grinned back, still catching her breath. "That's okay. I'm glad you did. I wanted to congratulate you, anyhow, but I never dreamed I'd get the chance."

He shrugged as if the compliment were meaningless to him now that the immediate thrill of victory had passed. Alex knew the feeling. For her the real victory was in her own knowledge of a perfectly executed dive. The judge's high scoring and the audience's applause, while important, didn't provide half the same thrill.

"It was pretty close," he said. "Ron Edwards is a real bulldog. He almost beat me." Alex smiled at the image he evoked. If she'd had to compare Wes to an animal it would be a bear, a shaggy lovable bear that could turn deadly with one flick of the paw.

"But you hung in there. Weren't you afraid?"

"Sure. I'm always afraid. That's what keeps me going. Adrenaline. Anyway, no one expects to get hurt until it happens to him . . . or her." He pulled off his gloves, tossing them aside as well. There was a grime-smudged refrigerator at the far end of the garage. Wes moved toward it, easily sidestepping the tools and tire rims that littered the cement floor amid puddles of old grease. "Do you want something to drink? I think there's some beer somewhere in here."

Alex laughed. "No thanks." She lifted a dripping strand of hair. "I think I've had enough." She remembered something Kit had told her. "You were hurt last year, weren't you?"

Wes shrugged it off, saying, "It wasn't much. A couple of broken bones. I was lucky. It could've been a lot worse." He paused, staring at her. "Hey, how come I haven't seen you around here before? Usually I see the same faces again and again. You've heard of rat races, haven't you? Well, around here we call the people who hang around tracks 'race rats.'"

"I guess I've been a closet fan." Quickly, she added, "Up until now, that is."

"Do you go to school around here?" West asked, sounding really interested. She didn't think he was just being polite.

"Glenwood High."

"No kidding?" His face lit up. "I used to go there myself. I graduated four years ago."

"That's when I started. I'll be graduating at the end of this year." Of course she would've remembered someone as exciting as Wes Thorsen if he'd still been at Glenwood when she started her freshman year.

"Small world." Wes clattered around in the fridge, unearthing a bottle of beer. An expert twist of the wrist against the corner of the workbench nearest him, and the cap flipped into the air. He was staring at her, those light green eyes sending shivers up the back of her neck. No boy had ever affected her like this since she'd become involved with Danny. But she still loved Danny, so it was crazy of her to feel this way. What did it mean?

Alex felt suddenly tongue-tied and a little shy. "Yeah . . . small world," she echoed weakly. Her knees suddenly felt incapable of holding her up, as if someone had come along and whacked them from behind with a baseball bat.

Wes seemed unaware of the effect he was having on her. "You look like the athletic type yourself," he said.

Alex was wearing her favorite orange jogging shorts and white T-shirt with the diving team's colorful emblem. Suddenly she became very conscious of what she must look like with her hair straggling about her face and her shirt stuck to her from a combination of champagne and perspiration.

"I'm on the diving team at school," she said. "But I've competed in some amateur meets, too. I hope I'll be able to make it into the Olympics someday."

"Hang in there and you will," Wes said, sounding very big-brotherly all of a sudden. His words reminded her of something Noodle had once told her: "Never say maybe. *You* have to believe you'll make it to the top, or nobody else's opinion is gonna get you there."

"I plan on it," she said. "You know, it's not that different from what you do. Only the thing about diving is, the person you're really competing against is yourself. If you want to be a winner you have to try and make every dive better than the one before."

Wes cocked his head to one side. The champagne foam had dried, and his hair corkscrewed out at cute angles. She saw in his eyes that he not only understood what she was telling him, but had experienced it himself. The corners of his mouth curled up in a slow smile.

"Gotcha," he said. He threw his head back, gulping down the rest of his beer. He tossed the empty bottle down beside his trophy. "Hey, listen, Alex, I'd like to . . ."

"Wes! I've been lookin' all over for you, buddy." A gray-haired man in greasy overalls stuck his head through the side door to the garage. He glanced at Alex, then back at Wes, sizing up the situation with a

104

sly wink. "I guess a pretty girl takes first place over a trophy any day. Next time just let us know where you're going when you duck out on us like that."

"Sorry, Max." Wes laughed, sounding not the least bit contrite. Alex could feel herself blushing. His incredible eyes twinkling, he added, "Alex and I had serious business to discuss. It just so happens she's an expert on winning technique."

The older man shook his head in amused disbelief. "Sure, Wes, whatever you say. But, look, if you can spare a few minutes, I've got some photographers waiting outside who for some dumb reason want pictures of your ugly face for the newspapers." He winked once more and disappeared, the door banging shut behind him.

"I guess I'd better go," Wes said.

But he didn't seem in any hurry to leave. He remained where he was, leaning casually up against the workbench, his laser-beam eyes fixed on Alex with an intensity that was having a strange effect on her. She wasn't sure whether she wanted to run in the other direction or throw herself at him.

Alex cleared her throat, which felt very dry all of a sudden. "Well, it was really nice talking to you." She laughed, plucking at her T-shirt where it lay pasted against her stomach. "And thanks for rescuing me, though I really didn't mind so much. It's not every day I get to take a champagne shower."

Wes started to walk away. Halfway to the door, he stopped and turned around. "Look, I hardly know you, so it's probably pushy of me to ask, but—would you like to go out sometime?"

Alex felt as if the air had been snatched right out of

105

her lungs. He was asking her out! This incredibly neat guy wanted to go out with *her*! Suddenly it was as if Danny didn't exist. She wanted to scream "Yes," to jump up and down, to skip out of the garage and shout the good news to her friends.

The exhilaration didn't last. Instantly, she sobered. How could she be even thinking about going out with someone else? She was in love with Danny, right? Being in love was serious business as far as Alex was concerned. She knew a lot of girls who said they were in love with a boy they were dating, but if someone better should come along . . . well, who knew? Alex wasn't like that. You either loved someone, or you didn't. There were no in-betweens.

Somehow, that left her more confused than ever. Because even though she *knew* she loved Danny, she couldn't seem to stop her heart from racing, or convince herself that she never wanted to see Wes again.

Alex shook her head regretfully. "I can't," she said.

Wes understood instantly. It was almost as if he could read her mind. "Boyfriend, right?"

She nodded. "Right."

"Well, it was a nice try. You can tell him for me he's a lucky guy. You're all right, Alex."

Did Danny feel lucky to be her boyfriend? Sometimes Alex wondered if he did.

"You, too," she said.

Wes merely shrugged, one corner of his disarming smile drooping ever so slightly. "Well . . . if you ever change your mind. You know where to find me."

"Where?"

Wes flung open the door. The small cluster of photographers who stood outside instantly descended on

106

him, their camera's flashing. He turned on the full force of his grin for their benefit before glancing back over his shoulder at Alex.

"In the newspapers!" he called out to her, laughing.

Alex waved to him as she took off in search of her friends, but he was so busy talking to reporters he didn't even notice. Would she ever see him again? She told herself it didn't matter, and that it probably would be better if she didn't see him. Still. She couldn't shake this feeling of restlessness that had come over her when she was with Wes. She'd never felt it before. And she knew, without a doubt, that if it hadn't been for Danny she *would* have accepted Wes's invitation.

Maybe this is how Danny felt about Stephanie? Still a bit dazed from her encounter with Wes, Alex groaned inwardly. If that were true then she had even more reason to worry than she'd thought.

# CHAPTER TEN

A car horn blared loudly in the early morning stillness. Alex stuck her head out her bedroom window and waved to Danny, whose blue Datsun pickup had just pulled into her driveway.

"Be out in a minute!" she called.

Danny waved back with his usual easygoing good-naturedness. He never seemed to be in a hurry, even if it meant they would be late.

Alex darted down the hallway, knocking sharply on Stephanie's bedroom, which was locked—as usual. "He's here! Better hurry up."

"Just a minute," came Stephanie's muffled reply.

Alex fidgeted with impatience. Why did Stephanie

have to be late? This wasn't the first time, either. Twice last week Alex had been late for school because she'd stupidly offered to give Stephanie a ride. And Stephanie hadn't even thanked her, much less apologized! She seemed completely unconcerned about putting people out and uninterested in what anyone thought of her.

Alex had packed her own belongings for the hike last night. Her navy-blue Alpine pack sat propped against the hatstand near the front door. It was six o'clock. She'd gotten up while it was still dark, and had already taken a shower, gotten dressed, and eaten breakfast. She was wearing her favorite old jeans and a red hooded sweat shirt over a tank top for when it grew warmer later on.

Stephanie wasn't even out of the shower by the time Alex had finished with everything. What on earth was she doing in there? Alex was sorry she'd ever invited her along on the hike, especially since there was no longer any reason for her to go. She couldn't figure out why Stephanie even wanted to—unless it was to be with Danny.

After what seemed like an eternity, the door swung open and Stephanie emerged. She wore jeans and an oversized sweat shirt and was carrying her ratty green backpack.

"Sorry," she said, not sounding it.

"I'll just say good-bye to Mom and Dad," Alex said. "They're still in bed, but I want to let them know we're leaving."

She knocked softly on her parents' closed bedroom door. Stephanie hung back. Alex could hear shuffling noises inside, then the door cracked open and her mother appeared, pulling on her bathrobe. Even with her hair tousled from sleep, she managed to look her usual perfectly composed self.

"Bye, Mom." Alex peeked over her shoulder at her father's sleeping form as she was giving her mother a kiss on the cheek. "Say good-bye to Dad for me. I'll see you tomorrow night. We should be back sometime before dark."

Stephanie didn't bother to say good-bye. She just stood there, pretending to be absorbed in adjusting the straps on her backpack. She hadn't allowed anyone in this family to get close to her, not even Mom.

"Stephanie?" Mom said softly, her dusky green eyes soft with unspoken concern. "Do you have everything you need? It might get cold. Did you pack that warm jacket I bought you last week?"

Stephanie stared at a spot on the wallpaper, frowning slightly. "I'll be okay. I'm used to taking care of myself."

Susan took a deep breath, tightening the belt on her blue robe. "Well . . . all right, then. I just thought . . . oh, well, never mind." She pasted on a bright smile. "Have fun, girls! I almost wish I were going with you, but I doubt I'd make it up the first hill."

Alex knew that wasn't true. Her mother was in great shape. She was very diet conscious and worked out three times a week at the Jack LaLanne spa at the shopping center. Part of the effect Noodle's illness had had on the family was to make everyone double aware of how precious one's health is.

But she couldn't help feeling a little annoyed at her mother as well. Why didn't Mom just let Stephanie have it once in a while, instead of putting on a smile and acting as if everything were perfectly okay?

Then her thoughts switched over to Danny, waiting patiently outside. She dashed for the front door, scooping up her backpack as she ran. Her sneakers squelched along the newly-cut grass of the front lawn, still damp with morning dew. She shivered in the chill air. The sky was the faded-denim color it got just before dawn.

Alex and Stephanie tossed their gear in back, then squeezed in beside Danny.

"Sorry we kept you waiting," Alex said. She felt uncomfortable talking to Danny with Stephanie beside her.

"That's okay," he said. He gave her a quick peck on the cheek. He smelled like soap and cornflakes, Alex thought, warming. He looked over at Stephanie, and smiled. "Hey, Steph, how's it going?"

"Fine," she said, casting a quick glance at Alex.

"How'd it go on that history test?" he asked.

"I got a ninety-eight," Stephanie said, beaming at him. "Thanks to your tips."

"It was nothing." He shrugged as he started the engine. "I took about fifty million of Mr. Barnett's multiple choice quizzes when I had him last year— that's how I happen to know his favorite tricks for tripping you up."

"Well . . . thanks, anyway."

Alex felt left out. She wondered why Danny was taking such an interest in Stephanie's schoolwork. Was he just being nice—or was it something more?

On the way over to the school, where they were meeting the other club members, they made trite small talk. For Alex, every word was a strain. She recalled how it had been on their last hike, on the drive to the mountains, when they had teased each other and sung silly songs. She'd made peanut butter sandwiches for the trip, and they'd had to gag them down because she'd forgotten to bring something to drink. Ever since then, neither of them could look at a peanut butter sandwich without laughing.

If only she and Danny could laugh now . . . or even fight. Anything but this awful, aching politeness.

Her thoughts were interrupted as Danny pulled into the Glenwood High parking lot. Already there was a cluster of cars, most of which would remain parked at the school over the weekend. Their supervisor, Mr. Webb, had arranged for the twenty kids going on the hike to divide up and ride in groups in the three largest vehicles, including Danny's truck and Peter Quist's Chevy van. Mr. Webb would lead the way in his camper.

It was a two-hour trip from Glenwood to the Santa Cruz mountains. Squeezed in between Danny and Joanne Burdick (fortunately, Stephanie had chosen to ride in back). Alex began to relax. After an hour or so, she grew sleepy. She leaned her head against Danny's shoulder. The hum of the car lulled her. The hilly road they were climbing, smooth and twisting, rocked her gently. Feeling so calm and cozy, it was easy to believe, then, that the reassurance of Danny's love she wanted so badly was just within reach. So close. Alex closed her eyes, imagining that everything was okay between them, just the way it used to be.

For one perfect moment, it seemed true. Suspended were thoughts of Stephanie . . . and of Wes Thorsen, whose rakish green eyes had been sneaking into her daydreams ever since that day at the racetrack. Danny loved her. She loved him. Everything would be okay.

"Getting tired?" Alex called over to Stephanie.

Stephanie seemed out of breath as she bent over, fiddling with her shoelaces. Her face was flushed with exertion. They had been climbing steadily for several hours, and the going was getting awfully steep . . . especially for a beginner not used to long hikes.

Through the dark strands of hair falling in front of Stephanie's face, Alex caught a glimpse of the frown she wore. "I'm fine," she said flatly.

"Do you want me to carry some of that stuff?" Danny asked, pausing beside her. "I warned you, it can get awfully heavy after the first mile or so."

Danny was panting only slightly. His shirt clung to his chest in dark wet patches where perspiration had soaked through. His face had the burnished rosy look of sunburn over a tan. Somehow, it made his eyes look bluer. They matched the color of the cloudless sky. He was wearing shorts; his long legs looked brown and strong.

Alex thought of the day of the senior picnic, when they'd hiked into the mountains and had made love that first time on a bed of dry pine needles. The memory sent a dart of pain shooting through her. They hadn't made love since that day up in his bedroom.

The trail Mr. Webb had chosen was stony and steep. It had taken them high up into rustling groves of Monterey pine and redwood trees. Their sharp, resiny fragrance filled the air. Pine needles covered the ground in a slippery cushion. The only sounds other than the crunching of their footsteps were the bicker-

114

ing of the birds hidden among the branches and the occasional mad skitter of a squirrel.

The rest of their group was slightly ahead—including Chuck Hadley, whom Stephanie had been avoiding since they'd arrived. She was the only real beginner of their bunch, so she was naturally slower. But since Mr. Webb had a rule about no one hiking alone, Alex and Danny had been forced to hang back and keep her company.

Stephanie hadn't complained, but it was obvious she was having a hard time keeping up even at the slower pace Alex and Danny had set. This was the fourth time since the hike began that she'd paused to tighten her shoelaces, which looked perfectly fine to Alex.

Stephanie straightened, flashing Danny a grateful look. "Thanks, but I can carry it. I didn't pack that much." She hoisted the frayed green straps of her backpack against her slender shoulders, falling in behind them as they trudged up the steep hill.

"It always feels like hell the first time," Danny said over his shoulder. "You get used to it after a while."

They'd been climbing only a few more minutes when Stephanie let out a yelp behind them.

Alex spun around. "What happened?"

Stephanie looked chagrined as she sat on the ground, holding her foot. "Nothing. I stepped on a rock."

Danny knelt beside her. "Let me see. These rocks aren't very sharp, I don't see how . . ." He stopped when Stephanie tried to jerk her foot away. It was too late. They saw the hole where the bottom of her sneaker had worn away.

Alex could no longer contain her exasperation. "Why didn't you say something? Mom and Dad would've given you the money to buy new sneakers!"

"There's nothing wrong with these!" Stephanie shot back defensively. "It's just a little hole. I didn't want a new pair. Anyway, I told you once before, I don't want anybody's charity."

"It's not *charity*, for heaven's sake. The state sends us an *allowance* for you." The instant Alex said it, she regretted it. She realized how it must have sounded—as if Stephanie were nothing more than a paid boarder.

Stephanie glared at Alex, her cheeks growing red. Hunkered down on the ground, cradling her foot, she looked so much like an angry, unloved child that Alex felt an instant's pity. But what good did it do? Stephanie didn't want her pity. Hadn't she told her that a hundred times?

Stephanie pulled herself up, and went over to sit down on a large flat rock sheltered by a low-hanging tree. "You two go on without me," she said in a strange tight voice. "I'll catch up later. My foot's fine, I just feel like having a smoke."

Alex bit her lip. "Look, Stephanie, I didn't mean—"

"Forget it," Stephanie interrupted. "Just forget the whole thing."

"Fine!" Alex said. "If that's the way you want it." She felt hot and irritable . . . and she was sick of Stephanie's bad moods. She turned to Danny. "Let's go. The others are already way ahead of us." She was determined not to let Stephanie ruin her whole afternoon.

Danny hesitated, which only succeeded in making

Alex feel more resentful toward Stephanie. "Maybe we should wait," he said. "Mr. Webb wouldn't like it."

Alex glared at him. "If you're so worried about Stephanie, then you stay with her. I'm not waiting around any longer!"

Danny ran after her as she was charging up the path, catching her arm. "What's got into you!" He sounded angry, and out of breath. "Look, I know Stephanie's hard to take sometimes, but you didn't have to blow up like that."

"Why don't you tell *her* that?" Alex cried, hurt. She pulled her arm from his grasp. Tears stung her eyes, but she blinked them back. "You're always on her side. You think I'm the one who's picking on her."

"Why do there have to be sides?" he asked.

"Go ask Stephanie. She's the one who's been against me ever since she moved in! And now she's turning you against me, too."

"That's ridiculous!" Danny shouted. "I'm not against you, Alex. I love you."

Alex felt as if he'd kicked her. She'd wanted him to say he loved her, but not like that. As she stared at him, his face melted into a watery blur.

"Do you, Danny? Do you?" she asked.

"Of course, I do!" His voice climbed. "If it's proof you want, okay—you win. I'll go with you."

She flinched. This wasn't turning out at all the way she'd wanted it to. Instead of feeling triumphant that Danny had chosen to go with her rather than stay with Stephanie, she felt worse than ever.

"Where's Stephanie?" Mr. Webb turned to Alex in the midst of taking a head count. It had been more

117

than an hour since Danny and she had rejoined the others, but she hadn't noticed that Stephanie was missing until now.

Alex scanned the group of hikers gathered in the small clearing where they'd decided to set up camp for the evening. "I thought she was right behind us." She looked over at Danny. "Have you seen her?"

"Isn't that her over there?" Danny pointed to a slender dark-haired girl in jeans with her back to them, also wearing an army-green backpack. From behind, she did look like Stephanie. Then the girl turned around, and they saw it was Melissa Haggarty. Danny frowned. "Well, I *thought* she was with us. After we caught up with everybody else, it was hard to tell."

Chuck Hadley came over. "What's going on? Somebody lost?"

"Stephanie," Alex said, feeling a stab of guilt. "Nobody's seen her in a while."

"I'm not surprised," Chuck snorted. "She doesn't strike me as the sociable type. Maybe she decided to head back on her own."

Some of the other kids wandered over and wanted to know what had happened. Everybody seemed concerned, even though they hardly knew Stephanie.

"We should go back and look for her," someone said.

"It'll be dark in a little while," Melissa pointed out. "We could get lost ourselves."

"I know where she might be," Danny said. "I remember the place where we left her. It was just below the bluff. There's no sense in all of us going."

"I don't like the idea of you going off on your own, Danny," said Mr. Webb. "Better pair up with someone

118

else. I'd go myself, but someone has to be in charge here."

"I'll go," Alex volunteered. She felt responsible. No matter how angry she'd been at Stephanie, she should never have gone off and left her like that.

Danny blamed her, too. Though he didn't say it, she could see it in his face as they started back down the slope. Halfway to the bottom, he stopped and turned to her.

"Go back," he said. "It's better if I go alone."

Alex stared at him. "Why?"

Danny's face was dark with shadows from the trees. It was almost night. "Let's just say I have a feeling she might not have gotten lost by accident."

"Mr. Webb wouldn't like it if we split up," she argued.

"He won't know until it's too late. Just tell him you turned your ankle or something."

He didn't give her a chance to argue any further. Sick at heart, Alex watched him turn abruptly and charge down the slope, going so fast his hiking boots kicked up a storm of pebbles that went skittering over the rocks below.

# CHAPTER ELEVEN

Alex felt as if she'd been waiting forever. It had been several hours since Danny had gone off in search of Stephanie. Every time she heard a noise coming from the darkness outside the big glowing circle of their campfire, she would jump up from her folded-over sleeping bag. But it was never them and she was sick with worry, unable to join in with the others who were toasting marshmallows and making s'mores with graham crackers and bits of Hersheys.

Alex knew that everybody else shared her concern as well. But they all had confidence in Danny's abilities as a skilled hiker. Mr. Webb was certain that Danny had done the smart thing, which was to make camp as soon as he'd found Stephanie, rather than trying to stumble their way back together in the darkness.

How could Alex admit that this was what worried her most of all? She, too, had confidence in Danny's ability to find his way back. What had thrown her into a panic was the thought of Danny and Stephanie out there somewhere alone . . . just the two of them . . . with no one but the stars and the moon looking over their shoulders . . .

Anything could happen.

Once again, she replayed in her mind the time she and Danny had made love out in the woods. It had been so wonderful. Almost magical. What if Danny tried to capture that magic again, only with Stephanie this time?

Alex felt sick at the thought. She had that awful achy feeling inside she got when she was coming down with the flu. *He wouldn't . . . he wouldn't,* she told herself.

*But Stephanie would.* The thought lodged in her mind like a sliver. The more she tried to dig it out, the more deeply it became wedged. Stephanie was capable of anything. She wouldn't hesitate to steal Danny away. Sometimes Alex wondered if it was really even Danny she wanted, or just the chance to strike out at Alex in any way she could.

She sensed that the cold war between her and Stephanie was just beginning to heat up.

It was past midnight when Joanne Burdick, one of the few still lingering about the fire, came over and sat down next to Alex. "Why don't you try and get some sleep?" she coaxed.

Alex burrowed deeper into her parka. High up on

the mountain, it got cold at night even during the warm spring months. Was Danny cold, too? Probably not. He and Stephanie had probably discovered lots of ways to keep warm.

Oh, God, why couldn't she stop thinking these thoughts?

"No, thanks," she told Joanne. "I think I'll sit up a little longer. I don't want to let the fire go out in case Danny's trying to find his way back." Even as she said it, her excuse sounded weak and improbable.

Joanne patted her arm in sympathy. "I know how you must feel. We're all a little worried. But I'm sure Danny's okay. And your friend, too. It's not like we're out in the wilds of the Amazon or anything. The worst that could happen to them would be to run into a poison oak bush in the dark."

Alex forced a smile. "Yeah . . . I guess you're right," she said, trying to sound cheered up. Joanne had no idea of the real danger involved.

"Get some sleep!" Joanne hissed as she crawled into her sleeping bag.

"I'll try."

Alex spent several minutes wrestling with the stuck zipper on her sleeping bag. Finally it gave, and she folded herself inside. Trying to fall asleep proved even more difficult. She lay on her back, staring up at the sky.

It was a beautiful night, crisp and clear. A full moon shimmered above the fringe of trees. A lover's moon. Her heart was so heavy, it felt as if a huge weight were sitting on her chest. Tears trickled down her temples into her hair.

Alex felt as if this night would never end.

Crunch.

Snap.

Alex's eyes flew open. The sky was milky white, a blank canvas waiting to be painted with the colors of the morning. But it wasn't the light that had awoken her; it was the sound of footsteps.

She glanced about, but the lumped-up sleeping bags surrounding her lay unmoving. Alex sat up. She was still dressed in her jeans and sweat shirt. Her eyes felt gritty, as if someone had glued sandpaper to the insides of her eyelids.

The rustle of footsteps among the deadfall came closer. Two shadowy figures appeared at the edge of the campsite. Alex leaped up.

"Danny!"

The huddled figures around her stirred. Tousled heads emerged one by one. Then suddenly the whole camp was awake, and everybody was swarming around Danny and Stephanie.

"Dr. Livingstone, I presume?" quipped Peter Quist, his sandy hair standing up in little peaks all over his head.

Danny broke out in a grin of happy relief. His sun-streaked hair was rumpled and had bits of bark and shredded leaves stuck to it. Stephanie looked as if she'd spent the night wrestling around on the ground as well. Her long dark hair lay tangled about her shoulders, stuck through with pine needles. Her brown eyes seemed to hold a satisfied, catlike glow.

"Hey, man, that was a neat trick you pulled, scaring

124

us like that!" Chuck cried, pounding Danny's back.

"Sorry about that," Danny said with a shrug. "But it was after dark by the time I caught up with Stephanie. We decided it'd be a lot easier to find our way back if we waited until it was light."

Alex felt like exploding. How could he treat the whole thing so lightly after all the torture she'd gone through? And why was he looking at Stephanie that way . . . as if the two of them shared some kind of intimate secret? Was it just her imagination, or had something really happened between them?

Alex was unable to keep from blurting: "You don't look too unhappy about it."

Danny shifted uncomfortably, his eyes not meeting hers. "I'm sorry if you were worried, Alex."

"I wouldn't have been so worried if you'd hadn't run off without me."

Stephanie spoke out in his defense. "It wasn't Danny's fault. I'm the one who got lost. I don't know what happened. I must have missed the path somehow."

*I'll just bet you did,* Alex thought. She was upset, as well as irritable, from lack of sleep. She glared at the hand curled on Danny's arm like a contented kitten.

Alex felt like slapping that sleepy smile off Stephanie's face, but just then Mr. Webb came over. He wanted to know every detail of the "ordeal," which didn't sound like much of an ordeal to Alex. She realized, however, that their director had been a lot more worried than he'd let on to her last night.

Alex was burning up, but she held it inside. She couldn't say anything now. Not with everyone else hanging around, listening. She waited until after breakfast, when they were packed up. On the hike down the mountain, she confronted Stephanie as soon as they were alone.

"What's going on with you and Danny?"

Stephanie's eyes narrowed. "I don't know what you're talking about. Nothing's *going on* between Danny and me."

"I don't believe you."

"Believe what you like." She yawned, lazily picking a pine needle from her hair. "Why should I care?"

Alex felt dizzy with anger. Heat climbed into her face. Even the roots of her hair felt as if they were on fire.

"That's right," she replied bitterly, releasing all her pent-up anger toward Stephanie. "I should have remembered. You don't care about anything. Or anyone."

"What difference would it make?" Stephanie demanded. "No one ever cared about me." She didn't sound as if she felt sorry for herself, just matter-of-fact.

"*I* cared. In the beginning, before . . . before all this."

"Who asked you to care?" Stephanie's voice cracked, becoming slightly shrill. A dry wind was blowing, whipping her long dark hair back from her face as she stood slightly hunched under the weight of her pack. "Who asked anyone in your dumb family to care? I don't want anyone to care about me!"

"Except Danny, right?"

"Danny's nice. And not because he has to be. He just is."

"Is that why you've been trying to take him away from me?"

126

Stephanie gave her a long, level look and said coolly, "I don't have to try and take Danny away from you, Alex. You're doing a good job of driving him away all by yourself."

Alex stared right back at Stephanie. She forgot all the reasons she'd felt sorry for Stephanie. She forgot about Stephanie's miserable childhood, and that horrible place she'd come from—Crestview Home for Girls. All she could think of was how nasty she'd been acting ever since she came to live with them; how she was practically ruining Alex's whole life.

"I hate you! I wish you'd never come to live with us!" Alex blurted hotly. "The whole thing was one big fat mistake!"

Stephanie flinched as if she'd been struck. Then her expression became very still, stonelike once again. Her only sign of emotion was the splotches of red that appeared on her pale face like a sudden rash.

But she only shrugged and said, "I could have told you that in the beginning."

Alex spent the drive home clenched in misery. She and Danny hardly spoke. It wasn't until he'd dropped off everyone else, and they'd driven out to a quiet place near the golf course, that they could talk about it.

"Nothing happened," Danny said.

He sat with his head bowed, pushing his thumb back and forth across a smudge of dirt on the steering wheel. He wouldn't look at Alex.

Alex eyed him closely. Suddenly, everything fell into place. She *knew*. "But you wanted something to happen, right?"

Danny didn't say anything. He didn't look up. The only sound was the rhythmic ticking of the engine as it cooled. They were parked on a hill overlooking the

Glenwood Acres golf course, a serene expanse so green in the sparkling late-afternoon sunlight, it hurt her eyes.

All of her hurt. She felt torn apart with pain, yet at the same time she was calm. It was the same kind of calmness she had felt when Noodle died, as if she'd known this was going to happen, and now that it had, she was relieved in a funny way.

"I'm not sure what I wanted. It wasn't the way you think," Danny said in a low voice. Finally, he turned slowly to look at her. His blue eyes were bright with anguish. "I guess what I liked about Stephanie was that she needed me. Not like you, Alex. You don't need me. Not really."

"That's not true! You've always been—"

"Second . . . to everything else in your life. And I don't mean just diving." His expression was full of pain. "Alex . . . what happened . . . I mean, what almost happened between Stephanie and me . . . it really wasn't because of *her*. It was because of us. We haven't talked about it, but you know what I mean. How we've been drifting apart lately. Maybe that's why we haven't talked about it. Because we knew what would happen if we ever did."

"No!" she cried, backing away from the raw, stinging truth of his words. She knew he was right; but that didn't stop her from not wanting to accept it. "Stephanie tried to steal you away from me! She hates me. She'd do anything to get back at me."

Danny shook his head. "You're wrong. Stephanie's not like that. Oh, I know how she acts. A real tough customer. But that's not how she is on the inside. I'm not defending her, I'm just telling it like it is. We're friends, that's all. Last night"—he paused—"well, it seemed like you and I had drifted so far apart in so many ways, and there she was. We talked about it. I think mainly what I felt was lonely. And Stephanie's lonely, too, no matter what she tells you. But we didn't do anything. Stephanie was the one who said we shouldn't. She said we didn't really love each other, and it was wrong to mix up friendship with love just because you're lonely. And besides, she wouldn't feel right about going behind anyone's back."

Danny's words cut into her, but Alex could no longer deny the truth in what he said. What surprised her though, was the part about Stephanie. Danny wasn't lying, she could see that. Besides, he was incapable of lying—that just wasn't his style. So she'd been wrong about Stephanie. She'd been so convinced by Stephanie's hard-core tough act that she'd allowed herself to believe it was more than skin-deep, that Stephanie really *was* as uncaring as she pretended to be.

She remembered something that had happened the first day Stephanie had come to live with them. Noodle's trophy. Stephanie had rescued it from the closet. She'd understood Alex's need not to have his memory entirely displaced. Even though she'd pretended her gesture was no big thing, Alex had realized then that it *was* a big thing.

Alex also recalled the horrible, hateful things she'd said to Stephanie that afternoon. She felt sick with guilt. No matter how badly her foster sister had behaved at other times, Alex had had no right to blame Stephanie for everything that had gone wrong between her and Danny.

129

Tears formed in Alex's eyes, but for once she didn't try to hold them back. She let them spill down her cheeks and didn't even bother to wipe them away.

"I guess I was trying to hide from the truth, too," she confessed shakily. "I knew we weren't getting along so hot—but it would've hurt too much to admit it."

She looked over and saw that Danny was crying as well. She'd only seen him cry once before—when Noodle died. A tear dripped from his chin onto the front of his T-shirt. His whole face sagged with misery.

"Oh, Alex," he choked. "I . . . I never wanted this to happen to us."

Alex took a deep, careful breath. Every part of her ached. It even hurt to breathe. She felt as if she might shatter apart like a crystal goblet if she made any sudden movements. Part of her didn't believe this was happening. In a way, it seemed more dreamlike than real. Yet she knew it was real. No dream could ever hurt this much.

"I think . . . maybe we're just too different." She was reaching out for an explanation, some sort of understanding. "We joked about it, but it wasn't always funny."

"No, I guess it wasn't." His hand slid across the seat, stopping inches from hers. "Alex, I've always felt I . . . well, that I was disappointing you, somehow. That you wanted me to be somebody I wasn't. More ambitious, maybe. The thing is—I can't be what you want. You can't change for someone, no matter how much you love them."

"You're right. I'm sorry, Danny." She moved her hand over so that her fingertips were just touching his. "You know, in some ways I wish I were more like you. I wish sometimes I could stop reaching, stop

130

wanting so much . . . just *stop*. You know what I mean?"

He nodded. "But that was always one of the reasons I loved you. This might sound sort of corny, but you really inspired me." He smiled. "When you weren't overdoing it."

Alex smiled back, as Danny handed her a tissue from the Kleenex box on the dashboard. Neither of them said anything. The silence stretched between them like a long hallway echoing with memories.

Finally, she said, "I guess this is it, huh?" She sniffed.

"I think it's sort of been over for a while," Danny replied. "I'll always love you, though. It just isn't the same anymore."

"I know. I felt it, too. But it's hard letting go. I'll always love you, too, Danny." She smiled through her tears. "It was good, wasn't it? In the beginning?"

"The middle, too." He cupped her chin, and kissed her gently on the cheek.

"We'd better stop before we make ourselves sick. This is starting to remind me of a Hallmark commercial." She tried to laugh, and the sob that was forming in her chest emerged as a hiccup.

"I'll remember that next time I want to buy you a birthday card." He paused. "Alex . . . do you think maybe . . . could we still see each other as friends?"

Alex thought it over. "No. It probably wouldn't be such a good idea. Not for a while. It's too soon. Being friends with somebody shouldn't hurt, and right now it hurts to be around you."

He nodded slowly. "Yeah . . . I think I know what you mean."

"Someday, maybe."

131

"We can write to each other when we're at college," he suggested.

Alex blew her nose in the tissue balled up in her fist. Then she let loose a long, shuddery sigh. It really was over. There was no turning back.

"Let's go home," she said.

# CHAPTER TWELVE

"Have you seen Stephanie?" Alex asked her mother when she got home.

Susan looked up from the pot roast she was sliding into the oven. "Oh, hi, honey! There you are. Dinner's almost ready. Tell Stephanie when you find her. She went out a few minutes ago. I thought maybe she was looking for you."

"Do you know where she went?"

"I've been in the kitchen since she got home. I just heard the front door a little while ago, so I assumed she'd gone out again. Maybe she's back. Have you checked her room?"

Alex raced into Stephanie's room. It looked the same

as it had on the day she arrived. Since then, she hadn't made one addition to the room except for the few things hanging in the closet and what was in the dresser drawers.

Unlike Alex's room, which had become a museum of clutter—everything from diving trophies to old ticket stubs—Stephanie hadn't put a single knick-knack on any of the shelves. There were no snapshots or scrawled memos stuck to the mirror. No stuffed animals on the bed. No half-read books or magazines scattered about the floor.

It looked, as Stephanie herself had once described it, like a room nobody had ever lived in.

Alex ran over to the closet and pulled it open. Empty. Only the hangers where Stephanie's clothes had hung were left, looking bleak and somehow accusing.

One by one, Alex wrenched open the dresser drawers. They, too, had been emptied of Stephanie's belongings. Suddenly, the realization of what had happened struck her full force. Stephanie had run away.

Guiltily, Alex recalled the awful words she'd blurted out in the heat of her anger this afternoon: *I hate you, I wish you'd never come to live with us.*

Where could she have gone? Alex searched her memory for clues. Stephanie didn't have much money, so she couldn't have gotten very far. Besides, it had only been an hour or so since Danny had dropped her off.

Alex decided not to wait around. Her favorite motto was: When in doubt, do something. Grabbing her car keys, she raced into the kitchen.

"I'm going out to look for her, okay, Mom? She probably just went to the drugstore or something. But

I need to talk to her." There was no point worrying her mother with the truth until she at least made an attempt to locate Stephanie.

It didn't look too hopeful, though. First, there was the problem of the Green Demon. Alex couldn't get it started. The engine revved a few times, then keeled over with a dying whine. No matter how many times she fixed this dumb car it remained as temperamental as ever.

By the time she finally got the Green Demon going half an hour later, it was dark. Alex shot out of the driveway . . . only to discover that only one headlight was working. Oh, well, she'd just have to hope she didn't get a ticket. That wasn't her biggest problem. Her biggest problem would be finding Stephanie. It wasn't easy finding someone in the dark with only one headlight . . . especially when that person didn't want to be found.

She tried the Greyhound bus station first—the most likely possibility. Her heart sank as she noticed a bus rumbling off just as she was pulling into the parking lot. But after talking to the ticket seller inside, she felt better. No one fitting Stephanie's description had bought a ticket for the 6:37 to San Francisco.

Alex checked the Wagon Wheel coffee shop, the pizzeria where Kit worked, even the library. No sign of Stephanie. Her panic mounted.

Cruising down Glenwood Avenue, Alex impulsively took the freeway exit leading to Highway One. Maybe because it was a favorite highway for hitchikers. Or maybe because it wound down along the coast, and Stephanie had told her once she liked being near the ocean.

She hadn't driven more than a mile when the beam from her single headlight picked up a lone figure trudging along by the side of the road. Alex saw a dark spill of hair, a ratty old army backpack. She slowed. The girl turned and put out her thumb. It was Stephanie.

Alex quickly pulled over on the wide dirt shoulder. Stephanie opened the door to the passenger side and stuck her head inside. She wore a sullen expression. "It's no use. I'm not going back. Tell your Mom and Dad thanks, but I just couldn't hack it."

Alex grabbed her arm. "Wait," she said. "Please, just get in for a minute. We don't have to go anywhere. I just want to talk."

"I don't see what there is to talk about," Stephanie replied. She didn't sound angry, just tired and resigned. But she got in anyway.

Alex shut the engine off. "We could talk about why you're running away, for one thing."

"That should be obvious. I don't stick around where I'm not wanted. Not"—she gave an airy wave of her hand and laughed, a dry, hollow laugh—"that I blame you. I know you tried. But, hey, it's like I told you in the beginning. I'm pretty much a loner. I don't want people doing me any favors."

"Who was doing you any favors?" Alex gulped. "We *wanted* you."

Stephanie ducked her head and started to get out. "Look, I've gotta go. I really can't stick around. It wouldn't work, anyway. It never does. It's not your fault. I just rub people the wrong way."

"What is it, Stephanie—are you afraid if you stick around you might get to like it?" Alex taunted, desperate to find some way of cracking through.

With Stephanie's head averted, all Alex could see was dark hair tangled across hunched shoulders. She couldn't tell whether Stephanie was angry, or merely indifferent.

Then Stephanie muttered, "Things go wrong when I'm around. They just do. Look what happened with Danny."

Alex flinched in pain at the thought of Danny. "What happened with Danny and me wasn't your fault." She stared down, picking at a thread that was unraveling from the seat. "I guess I just wanted to think it was. Why didn't you tell me what happened last night?"

"Would you have believed me if I had?"

"I don't know," Alex answered honestly. "Maybe. The point is, you *wanted* me to think something had gone on between you two, even though you were denying it. Why?"

Stephanie shrugged. "It was easier."

"I don't get it," Alex said. She wanted to understand, but Stephanie wasn't helping any.

"I know what you think of me. I figured it was easier for you to blame me than Danny."

"Are you in love with him?"

She shook her head. "I probably could be. He's really special, you know."

Alex swallowed hard. "I know."

"Look, I may be a lot of things, but I wouldn't do anything like that. Maybe because I've had enough people dump on me, I know how it feels. I never tried to steal Danny away from you."

"I suppose it's always easier to blame someone else." Alex sighed. "What happened with Danny and me . . . well, it was nobody's fault." She stared at

Stephanie. "Is that why you're running away, because you thought I blamed you?"

"I told you. I never stay in one place for long. It gets boring."

"I don't believe you. I think you've been running away ever since you got here. You won't give us a chance because you're afraid you might like us and *want* to stay. Isn't that it?"

Stephanie whipped about, her dark eyes luminous with tears, the watery greenish light from the dashboard playing over her pale face. "You think you know so much. I'll tell you about the foster families I've had. The first one I went to live with, after my mother ditched me—I wanted them to like me real bad. I even called them Mom and Dad. Dad Jenkins—he's the one who beat me up. Then they sent me to live with another family. They were even nicer. The told me straight up front they were only taking me in for the money. It wasn't so bad then. At least I knew the score." Her words spilled out in a hard, angry rush. "You want me to take chances? I'll tell you what taking chances means to me. It means getting hurt. Do you know what it's like to want to be part of a family so bad that you—" Her voice broke. With what appeared to be a tremendous effort, she brought her trembling body under control, stiffening her shoulders, gathering her anguish into a hard knot. "Oh, hell, what's the use? All of that stuff happened a hundred years ago. Who cares, anyway?"

"I do," Alex said softly, realizing as she said it that it was true. Stephanie was a fighter. She'd had to be in order to survive all those awful experiences. She just didn't know when to stop fighting.

Anguish broke through once again in Stephanie's voice. "Who asked you to care?"

"Nobody! I care because I'm a person, and people just can't help caring about each other . . . even if it means getting hurt. Look, I know you've had some bad experiences. But that doesn't mean it's going to all turn out bad. *I'm* not giving up on you"—she jokingly held up a fist—"even if it kills us both."

Stephanie stared at Alex for a long, tense moment, obviously struggling to hold her mask in place. She began to shake, then all at once the mask crumbled into a thousand fragments. Her expression melted in anguish. She covered her face with her hands and started to sob—harsh, barking sobs that sounded as if they were being ripped out of her against her will.

Alex's own eyes welled with tears. She wanted to put her arms around Stephanie and console her the way she would have if it had been one of her friends—Kit, Elaine, or Lori. But she held back, sensing it was too soon. They had a long way to go in their journey toward trusting each other. For now, it was enough to know there was still a chance.

"It won't be perfect," Alex warned her. "There'll be plenty of times we'll fight and probably even hate each other. But I won't give up on you. And no more blind dates, either. I promise."

Stephanie raised a swollen face to Alex. "I'm sorry I blew up that time," she said. "You just caught me by surprise, that's all. I wasn't expecting it. I don't like surprises too much, since most of the ones I've had haven't been good."

"It was mostly my fault," Alex confessed. "I should've told you. I just didn't think I could've gotten you to go out with Chuck any other way."

"You could have asked me."

"Would you have said yes?"

Stephanie shook her head, a small smile creeping in. "Uh-uh. He's not my type. I think Paula would like him, though."

They both laughed.

"Okay?" Alex said. "Will you give us a chance?"

Stephanie turned away, and for a moment Alex thought she might be slipping away again. Then she said in a small, thin voice, "I don't know how to . . . I've never had a real family . . ."

Alex touched her shoulder. "You do now."

Stephanie looked at her. She didn't have to say how she felt. It was in her face. The look of hardness was gone, and in its place was an expression of shy, tentative trust.

On the way back to the house, they didn't speak. Alex guessed that Stephanie felt as embarrassed as she did about revealing so much all at once. It had been hard to do, even if it was for the best.

Suddenly, she remembered about dinner. She'd promised Mom she'd be back in time for the pot roast that had been in the oven when she left. But that was hours ago. Mom and Dad had probably eaten already and were worried sick.

"How do you feel about cold pot roast?" she asked Stephanie.

"Ugh." Stephanie made a face.

Alex laughed, mostly in relief. The tension was broken. "I'm glad to see we have one thing in common," she joked. "A mutual hatred of cold pot roast."

140

"You're weird, Alex. Really weird. Did anyone ever tell you that?"

"Sure, plenty of times. You're pretty weird yourself, you know."

"Me? You just don't recognize supreme cool when you see it."

"Ha!"

A moment later, Stephanie asked, "Is this the way sisters fight?"

They grinned at each other.

"How should I know?" Alex growled. "I never had one . . . until now."

# CHAPTER THIRTEEN

"There are certain things you should never stoop to, no matter how brokenhearted you are," Lori said with a sigh, gazing mournfully at the framed photograph of Perry on her dresser—all she had left of him now that he'd moved away.

It had been several days since Perry had left, and this was the first time all of them had gotten together for one of their marathon summit conferences. It was Lori who had suggested a sleep-over, complaining that if she had to spend one more night alone mooning over Perry, she might end up drowning in her own tears.

"Like what?" Alex asked.

"Like kissing your boyfriend's picture," Lori said.

"Is that why there are lipstick smudges all over it?" Kit teased. She lay sprawled on her stomach on Lori's bed, wearing her favorite slinky red harem pajamas.

Lori blushed. "Just because I said I shouldn't, doesn't mean I *didn't*. Anyway, it's better than eating a whole bag of Oreos, which is what I almost did."

"You're absolutely right," Elaine said. "Hey, are there any left?"

She'd been painting her toenails a pale pearly-pink. Now she stumped about the room on her heels, feet splayed, with tufts of cotton sticking up between each toe, as she waited for them to dry. Alex couldn't help smiling at the picture she made, waddling around in her pink flannel nightshirt with her hair rolled up in curlers. She looked like a flamingo.

Lori's blush deepened. "About three, I think," she confessed, shrinking into the white rattan chair she was sitting on. Dressed in a flowered granny gown that fell to the floor, with her hair gathered up in a loose topknot, she resembled one of those languishing Victorian ladies Alex had seen in paintings.

"Boy, I'm starved!" Kit cried.

"We could send out for pizza," Stephanie suggested shyly. She was obviously enjoying herself, but she still hung back from joining in too much. She reminded Alex of someone learning to swim for the first time— the first thing you had to master was how to float. That was what Stephanie was doing, floating, testing the water.

Elaine grinned. "Sounds good to me."

"I could probably get Justin to bring one over," Kit said. "He's working at Gennaro's tonight." She sighed. "It's probably the only chance I'll get to see him all weekend. Between his job and his training sessions at the lab, we're practically strangers. I just know I'm going to call him up one day, and he's going to say, 'Kit who?'"

"At least you get to see him sometimes," Lori pointed out. "That's better than *never* . . ." She sniffed, pulling out the Kleenex that was tucked into the elastic of her ruffled sleeve.

"I know how you feel," Alex said. "I miss Danny, too." She curled deeper into the bean bag chair she occupied in the corner, by Lori's ruffled vanity table. It hurt talking about Danny this way. She still had a hard time believing they had actually broken up.

"Do you think you two will get back together?" Elaine wanted to know. She stopped her funny duck-walk and sank down on the bed beside Kit. She looked over at Alex.

Alex shook her head. "No. It's funny . . . I miss him, but I know it's better this way. We're really so different that it's a miracle we stayed together as long as we did."

"It must have been because you loved each other," Lori said.

"That's true," Alex said. "We did."

She had a brief image of Danny and herself nestled together on a bed of pine needles, the sun warm against their bare bodies. The memory sent a sharp pain flashing through her. Despite how hard it was going to be to get over Danny, she was glad they'd broken up while they still had good feelings about each other, while the good memories outweighed the bad.

Lori had gone back to staring dreamily at Perry's picture. "I keep thinking about our last night together. How special it was . . ."

Uh-oh, Alex thought, here it comes. She's going to confess that she and Perry went to bed together. Poor Lori! No wonder she was suffering so much.

". . . We had dinner here. I made everything—I even baked him a chocolate fudge cake, his favorite. Mom was out, so we had the whole house to ourselves. It was so romantic . . ."

"Lori, you *didn't!*" Kit jackknifed into a sitting position. She leaned forward, elbows on knees. Obviously, she was thinking the same thing Alex was.

Lori blinked in innocent surprise. "Didn't what?"

Alex stared at her. "*You* know."

"Oh, *that.*" Lori's cheeks were bright red as she shook her head. "We decided not to after we talked about it. Perry said I might regret it afterwards, and maybe even hate him for it. I know that would never have happened, but I'm glad we didn't, anyway. It was too soon in a lot of ways . . . and maybe too late in others." Her blue eyes shimmering with tears, she pulled out from under her nightgown a gold locket fastened to a chain around her neck. "He gave me this to remember him by instead."

They all got up and crowded around to take a closer look. It was so perfect, Alex thought. Only someone who knew and loved Lori well could have chosen such an ideal gift for her. Inside the delicate gold locket was engraved:

"Love you always, Perry."

Elaine sighed wistfully. "If Carl ever gives me some-

146

thing to remember him by, it'll probably be a microchip."

Kit giggled. "With Justin, it'll probably be a bronzed pizza."

Stephanie joined in on the joking. "The only present I ever got from a boy was when Davey Gottlieb gave me a Whoopi Cushion in the fourth grade." She grinned. "But that was only after I left rubber barf on his chair."

They all cracked up, laughing until tears ran down their faces as they exchanged stories, each one more outrageous than the next. It was pure silliness. But Alex had discovered that silliness was often the best cure for misery.

When their giggles had subsided, they trooped into the kitchen, foraging among the cupboards and refrigerator for snacks. Lori unearthed the rest of the Oreos, a box of Wheat Thins, some cheese, and the crumbled remainder of the chocolate fudge cake she'd made for Perry.

They carried it all out into the living room, where they devoured every crumb while watching an old Bette Davis movie on television. Halfway through the movie—which was all about Bette Davis bravely carrying on through every kind of possible ordeal, including losing the man she loves—Lori turned to Alex.

"Do you think we'll ever fall in love again?" she asked.

"I hope not." Alex laughed.

"You will," Kit said knowingly. "Look at my mother. She's been in love so many times, I'm surprised she hasn't burned out on men completely."

" 'Hope springs eternal,' " quoted Elaine.

Alex groaned. "That's what I'm afraid of." But even though she felt scared by the prospect of falling in love again, she had to admit, if only to herself, that she wouldn't mind dating someone just for fun.

"I could never feel the same about anyone else," Lori declared staunchly. "No one will ever take Perry's place."

"You feel that way now, but it'll change," Elaine said. "Remember how crazy you were about Mr. Castellano?" Mr. Castellano was Lori's art teacher at Glenwood, whom she'd had a terrible crush on for a while. Older men seemed to hold a deadly fascination for her.

"For a while, every time you sketched a guy he ended up looking like Mr. C," Kit recalled with a smile. "Now they all look like Perry."

"Hey, wouldn't it be cool if it worked the other way around?" Stephanie said. "Like, you could draw a picture of your dream man, and then tack it up on the bulletin board at school. Like those *Wanted* posters they had in the Old West."

Alex smiled as she munched on a cracker. "Usually, it doesn't work that way. When you look for love, you can never find it . . . then just when you've given up, wham! It strikes."

"And usually knocks you flat," added Kit.

"It's sort of scary when you think about it," Lori said. "I mean, how little control we have over it. I suppose in some ways it's like getting struck by lightning."

"Only with lightning, you never get struck twice," Elaine said.

"Maybe the trick is to run fast enough so that it won't get you," Alex said.

"Need a hand?" Alex addressed the pair of legs sticking out from under the car.

On impulse, she'd stopped by the racetrack on her way home from school. Wes probably wasn't even around, she'd told herself. But even if he was, it wouldn't hurt just to say hello, would it?

She'd found him in the garage, working under his car. Well, half of him, anyway.

Wes's upper half emerged: broad shoulders, sparkling green eyes, rumpled black hair—in that order. He wore a pair of old green coveralls like the ones she had at home. There was a smudge of grease on one cheek. Alex felt the muscles in her knees go weak.

When he saw her, his face lit up with a broad grin. "Hey! Alex! I didn't think I was going to see you again. Don't tell me you've become a race rat."

Alex laughed. "Not quite. I was just driving by, so I thought I'd stop in and say hello." She could feel herself growing warm. "But I wasn't sure you'd remember me."

Wes scrambled to his feet. "Are you kidding? How could I forget? You're the only girl I know who likes taking showers in champagne."

Alex laughed. "I never do things the ordinary way. It keeps my life from getting too dull."

"I know what you mean. I'm the same way."

Staring into Wes's green eyes. Alex went all tingly with a mixture of fear and anticipation. Now what? Where did she go from here? Suppose he asked her out again? She wasn't sure how she felt about dating someone so soon after her breakup. What she and Danny had shared had been so real, so strong, it would be a while before she could open herself to that kind of love again.

"Am I interrupting you?" she asked, glancing over at his car.

"Nah. I was just making a few adjustments. I'm finished now." He kicked shut the toolbox that sat on the concrete floor beside the car. He looked at her, his gaze dancing over her face. "Say, do you feel like going for a ride? I was going to test her out on the track."

Alex leaped at his invitation. "I'd love it!"

"We'll be going pretty fast. I hope you're not the squeamish type." His green eyes held a hint of challenge.

Alex tossed her head back and laughed as a wild rush of abandon swept through her. Why not? The faster, the better.

"Try me," she said.

# YOUNG Love®

## IS A VERY SPECIAL FEELING